THE GREEN MAN RETURNS

By
HAROLD M. SHERMAN

I0616859

ARMCHAIR FICTION
PO Box 4369, Medford, Oregon 97504

*The original text of this novel was first
published by Ziff-Davis Publishing*

*For more information about Armchair Books and products, visit our
website at...*

www.armchairfiction.com

Or email us at...

armchairfiction@yahoo.com

THE LAST CHANCE FOR EARTH?

The Great Light came to Earth as the Green Man had said—and there was no war…

In this tongue-in-cheek, often moralistic sequel to "The Green Man," Numar of Talamaya returns to tell the world of his far-reaching plan to change Earth into an eternally peaceful planet. A galactic citizen of wide-spread magnitude, Numar predicts the destruction of Earth if his instructions are not carefully adhered to.
Numar's comprehensive plan is based on a socialistic culture where all the planet's citizens are essentially equal. The problem he faced, though, was enlisting the cooperation of those people on the higher end of Earth's social spectrum. Would he succeed, or would Earth's destruction become imminent? Find out in this wild, satirical tale from the pages of Raymond A. Palmer's Amazing Stories *magazine.*

CAST OF CHARACTERS

NUMAR aka THE GREEN MAN
He was the man with the plan. If Earth was to survive, its peoples would have to follow his instructions.

GRANDMA BETTY HOPPER
While all the world waited in fear this woman was rejoicing— knowing only that the Great Light's coming had been foretold.

ELLEN HOPPER
She had heard tales of The Green Man throughout much of her life. Now she had a tale of her own tell.

PETROV GOUCHEVISKY
Handsome and debonair, this Russian attaché had a captivating manner and charm—but was his winsome personality a sham?

ANDREW BROWNELL
A troubleshooter for the government, he was all business. But what kind of trouble brought a man of his stature to his knees?

GENERAL MONIHAN
He had a sneaking suspicion that relations with Russia were going downhill fast. And, brother, was he ever right!

KATHERINE BARKER
This woman's jealously was about to get the whole world destroyed. Honestly…women can be so catty!

CHAPTER ONE

NINETEEN Hundred and Seventy-five will be known forever to the inhabitants of this earth as the Year of the Great Light.

It was seen first by the startled peoples of the Eastern Hemisphere. Word of this tremendous illumination, which turned night into day, spread quickly by radio to the millions of humans on the other side of the globe. They awaited its manifestation with growing feelings of terror as continued reports and descriptions of this heavenly phenomenon gave rise to the fear that the end of the world was at hand.

This Light was appearing in the east as the sun was setting in the west. Observers said it started first in what seemed to be a new and brilliant early evening star, the luminosity of which rapidly and vastly expanded while yet one looked. Shadows left by the departing sun were swept away by the onrush of this tremendous beam of Light, which lit up the countryside with an awesome white glow. No other stars could be seen, not even the moon. The heavens themselves were invisible. As one looked upward, all he saw was dazzling brightness. Strangest of all, the Light was without heat.

In the capitols of Moscow, Chunking, Berlin, Paris, Rome, London and Washington, there was wild consternation for it was in these capitols that the Third World War was being plotted. At secret Army air bases and rocket atomic bomb sites, orders were even now being awaited to launch undeclared warfare. Mighty Soviet Russia and her satellites against the United States, Great Britain and their allies in an intended final test of power to determine the destiny of all humans for all future time.

And now—The Great Light. What could be its cause? What is its meaning? What is its foreboding? Until these questions could be answered there could be no further thought of war. Mankind was being threatened by a possible cosmic catastrophe so colossal as to strike fear into the hearts of rulers and common people alike.

In Washington, high officials gathered on the steps of the Lincoln Memorial at dusk to get their first view of this weird astronomical happening. While the President and his aides were watching from an elevation in the White House, all over Washington, as in all eastern cities and communities of the United States, Canada and South America, humans were looking skyward. They wanted to see what already had been seen by teeming millions in Europe and Asia, yet many trembled and shook as they saw the sun sinking from sight and knew that the moment for their vision of The Great Light had arrived.

The radio networks of the country had been set up to carry the word picture of this unprecedented phenomenon as it traversed the surface of the earth, from east to west, with the passage of time.

FOR some strange reason this Great Light, unlike the magnetic disturbances caused by the Aurora Borealis and occasional electrical storms produced by sunspots, had no effect upon radio transmission or reception. Excited reports had been coming in from foreign observers for some hours. Even now a broadcaster from London was saying:

"It is past one o'clock in the morning, Greenwich, England time, and you people in America and the Western Hemisphere should soon be sharing this tremendous astronomical experience with us.

"As I am talking, the brilliance of this illumination is flooding the broadcasting studio. It is actually lighter than day. We have the eerie sensation that this is just the prelude to some unimagined occurrence.

"Numerous suicides are now being reported. Humans all over England, and I dare say everywhere else where this Light has appeared, are flocking to the churches. There is no one asleep in the Eastern Hemisphere tonight. All emergency services are organized and standing by to take whatever action may be necessary or possible.

"I confess to a feeling of utter futility and helplessness. It seems as though this Light is searching out not only the dark and forbidding places of earth but also the dark corners of men's minds. Most certainly it causes you to examine your own self and to wonder what fate may await..."

The broadcast was broken off by intervention of the American networks.

"Here it comes, ladies and gentlemen!" an announcer's voice cut in. "This is Carl Rand reporting from the top of the Empire State building in New York. The sun has just disappeared beneath the horizon across the Hudson and dusk is falling but, as I look toward the east, I see a strange white glow and streamers of light beginning to extend into the sky.

"Far below me, the lights of New York City have begun to blink on. Broadway's Great White Way is a blaze of Neon. As far as I can see there is a checkerboard of streetlights. But apparently our man-made illumination won't be needed for long if this heavenly manifestation is to be like that experienced abroad.

"The roofs of buildings everywhere are jam-packed with humans. I doubt if any theaters or nightclubs are doing business at this moment. Many people, through fear, are hiding in subways, in other dark recesses or in closets or basements of their homes.

"While I have been talking, these weird streamers of white light have been rapidly fanning out. At this instant they resemble, on a cosmic scale, the Kleig lights of a Hollywood premiere. But not for long, ladies and gentlemen. These streamers have fused into a solid wall of luminosity, which now seems to be advancing toward us, lighting up every object on earth.

"Oh! This is sensational! Parts of Long Island, Brooklyn, Queens and surrounding country are standing out, bright as day. It's just as though some mammoth searchlight is being turned on the world. Now it's hitting closer—the ocean is glistening like a mirror. There's Coney Island, lit up so plainly I can see the outlines of the beach. Now the Light's hitting New York, catching the higher buildings first. The Tri-Borough and Brooklyn bridges... Oh! I can't keep up with it... It's spreading everywhere. It's right over us! This Observation Tower is bathed in it...

"Looking up I can't see anything but Light! Looking down, you wouldn't know that man-made lights were on. This Great Light is now advancing across the Hudson, driving all darkness before it. There is the George Washington Bridge—the Palisades—oh! They are magnificent under this Light... Even the smallest things stand out, miles away.

"But, most awe-inspiring of all, as I'm gazing over New York, are the millions of upturned faces. I'm not conscious of a sound. It seems as though the whole world is holding its breath.

"And now, ladies and gentlemen—there is Light *everywhere!* I can't describe my emotions. There just aren't any words to tell how you feel when this Light hits you. I want to pray; I want to scream; I want to run away. It's not real—and yet, it's happening!

"This is Carl Rand, returning you to the network to which you are listening for the next on-the-spot broadcast of this stupendous phenomenon..."

IN WASHINGTON, a boy of seventeen stood at the end of the Lagoon near the Lincoln Memorial in the company of his parents. His eyes were fixed on the eastern horizon as the first glow of The Great Light appeared.

"What do you think it is, Dad?" he asked.

Senator John Henry Ransom, from Arkansas, shook his head. "I don't know, son. Some of the old folks up in our hills would say it was 'the Lord comin' for to fetch His own.'"

"But it's not anything like that," said Helen, the boy's mother. "The Lord doesn't do things that way."

The lad's face was thoughtfully serious. "He'd better do something pretty quick," he said, as he watched the sky. "This world's a mess!"

Around and about the Ransoms stood a great crowd of Washingtonians from every walk and run of life. They were all tormented by the same pulsating question: What force in the Universe was behind this? Did this Light have any spiritual significance? Or was the Cosmos, in a catastrophic mood, preparing to erase puny Man and thus end his sorry history of ages-old inhumanity forever?

There was one elderly woman in LaCanada, California, suburb of Los Angeles, who—of all humans on earth—was not frightened by the appearance of the Great Light, who even welcomed it as fulfillment of a prophecy, which she recalled, had been made to the world years ago.

Just last week, when asked by her grandchildren to tell them a story, Grandma Betty Hopper had wiped the mist off her bifocals, settled back in hear easy chair and said: "Wait, children. I guess you're old enough now for me to tell you about the wonderful Green Man who came here one time from another planet—and the prediction he made—which I think, some day, is going to come true."

"Oh, Granny," protested Harry Hopper, the III, aged six, "don't give us any of that old 'Buck Rogers stuff.' That's out of date."

"I'll say it is," supported bright-eyed Annabelle, aged five. "There's never been any Green Man here."

Grandma Hopper clicked a set of the best plastic teeth in America to curb her exasperation. "That's just the trouble with you children of today," she said. "You don't believe any thing-—even when it's true—as this is."

Harry Hopper, the III, eyed her with the mature skepticism of all his six years. "All right, Granny," he accepted. "Go ahead. Tell us about your Green Man. We'll listen—but it had better be good."

Grandma Hopper brushed a wisp of graying blonde hair from her face and looked off into the distant past. "I was a young girl then," she said, "and if I do say so myself—I was mighty good looking. In fact, I had what was commonly referred to in those days as 'sex appeal.'"

"You can skip that," said Harry, the III, "and get to the Green Man."

"No," insisted Grandma Hopper, "that's important because it got me my chance for a screen test in Hollywood. Oh, I suppose I had a little acting ability, too, but as I look back, I can see it was my face and figure that did it."

"*I've* got a good face and figure, haven't I, Granny?" asked Annabelle. "Daddy says I look just like your baby pictures."

"Yes, dear—if your grandfather had only lived to see what an image of me you are…"

Annabelle's blonde head nodded. "Well, he *would* have, if he hadn't tried to fly to the moon, wouldn't he?"

GRANDMA HOPPER sighed. "I don't know, dear. Your grandfather was the most dare-devilish man I ever knew. There wasn't a thing he couldn't do with an airplane—and I just couldn't keep him from volunteering for that first manned rocket trip. He'd led such a charmed life that he actually believed he could make it to the moon and back. I think he figured if a Green Man could come here in a space ship that he should be able to go places, too. Well—he didn't succeed, but some day, when Man has conquered space, your grandfather's name will head the list as the first human who ever tried to do it."

"Gee," exclaimed Harry, the III. "I didn't know, Granny—did Grandpa see the Green Man, too?"

"Of course he did. And the Green Man told him that we would be married and that, one day, we'd be telling of his visit to our children and our children's children." Grandma Hopper touched a handkerchief to her eyes. "His prediction wasn't so far wrong. We both told your father and your Aunt Ellen—but now I'm having to tell you, *alone.*"

Harry, the III, seated himself on the floor beside his wide-eyed sister, at last prepared to give respectful attention.

"I was in New York when I got my chance to go to Hollywood," Grandma Hopper went on. "I was engaged to your grandfather then but our country was at war and Uncle Sam had taken him to a flying field in Texas. I remember how disappointed I was that we both couldn't have gone to Hollywood together, for your grandfather had dreamed of being a great actor. But the war changed all that—and here I found myself on a plane, bound for Los Angeles."

"What *make* of plane was it?" asked Harry, the III.

"Mercy, child," said Grandma Hopper, "how should *I* know? It was a regular transport such as they had in those days."

"Did it go faster than sound?" asked Harry.

"No, of course not. I don't think it went more than two hundred and eighty miles an hour."

"As slow as that?" said Harry. "Gee, Granny—that's not as fast as the rocket trains go today."

Grandma Hopper gave a snort of irritation. "Do you want to hear about the Green Man or don't you?" she demanded.

"I'm sorry," said Harry, contritely. "Go on. Let's get to him."

"I'm getting there just as fast as you'll let me. You see, I had a favorite Aunt and Uncle who lived in this very town you live in and in this very house."

"You mean—our Great Great Uncle William?" asked Annabelle.

"Yes, dear," said Grandma Hopper. "He wasn't only your Great Great Uncle, but Professor William Bailey was a great astronomer in his day."

"Did he know Mars was inhabited?" asked Harry.

Grandma Hopper made an effort to hold her patience. "No, Harry—that hadn't been discovered yet."

"Well, gee—he didn't know much, then. When are we going to get to this Green Man?"

"Pretty soon now. Be quiet." Grandma Hopper leaned forward, and her face took on a look of excitement. "I can see it all just as though it were yesterday. I'd planned to surprise my Uncle and Aunt and go right to their house from the airport. I knew they'd be glad to have me stay with them, but when I got there I found their only guest room was taken, and I was the one who was surprised. Their visitor was a man from Space!"

"The Green Man?" asked Harry. How'd he get there? Where'd he come from? What'd he look like?"

GRANDMA HOPPER smiled. "He came in his own space ship. He said his name was 'Numar, from the planet Talamaya,' which was located over a trillion miles away in the direction of our Milky Way, and he was over six feet tall and wore a white robe and a tight-fitting headdress…and his skin was *green!"*

"Green all over?" asked Harry.

"Well, naturally. Of course I never saw him all over. What a question!"

"Did Great Great Uncle William see him all over?" persisted Harry.

"Why, I don't suppose so. He'd have had a pretty hard time doing it. Mister Numar never went to bed. He never slept the whole week he was here. Not only that, he never ate a mouthful of food…all he said he needed was air and water."

"And you believed all that?" scoffed Harry. "Granny, were *you* simple…"

"If I was," countered Grandma Hopper, "I had lots of company. Your Great Great Uncle William believed in the Green Man and so did your Grandfather when he finally met him—and quite a few other people, too. You see, the reason the Green Man couldn't eat food was because he didn't have any stomach."

"No stomach?" cried Annabelle, who had been listening with fixed interest. "How could anybody live without a stomach?"

"The Green Man did. He wasn't human. He had different organs that generated electricity from the water he drank and the air he breathed. If he wasn't careful he gave people a terrible shock whenever they touched him or shook his hand. I kissed him once and I can feel that shock yet."

Harry surveyed his grandmother, critically.

"Hadn't you ever been kissed before?" he asked.

"Now, Harry—after all—I told you I was a beautiful young lady and I naturally—well—your grandfather had kissed me dozens of times—but kissing the Green Man was different. It felt like millions of needles running through me—from my lips right down to the tips of my toes—almost like being electrocuted."

"Did the Green Man kiss anybody else?" queried Harry, with deep clinical interest.

Grandma Hopper laughed. "No, once was enough for him. You see—he'd never kissed before." Then, as she saw her grandson's look of incredulity, she added: "They didn't kiss on his planet."

"Why not—was it prohibited?"

"They never thought of it, I guess—no—that couldn't be the reason—" Grandma Hopper was suddenly perplexed.

"Maybe they rubbed noses like the Eskimos do," suggested Annabelle.

"Well," decided Grandma, "they did *something*—we can count on that—but it has nothing to do with my story."

Harry shook his head. "If the Green Man had no stomach—how do you know—?"

"Harry, I am not an authority on the Green Man's anatomy, so you must not plague me with questions. I'm telling you all I know. He said he'd been alive some millions of years and that the beings on his planet had been watching our development here."

Harry glanced sidewise at his sister, Annabelle.

"Do you believe this stuff?" he demanded.

"Why, of course," said Annabelle, with a loyal look at her grandmother. "Everything Granny tells us is so."

"All right, then—how could the Green Man tell what was happening on our earth a trillion miles away?" challenged Harry.

"Why, they had instruments much more powerful than our telescopes," explained Grandma Hopper, "and they've been able to observe and study everything we've been doing here for ages."

"That's the Green Man's story," said Harry. "But how can you prove it?"

"I can't," admitted Grandma Hopper. "But I've never doubted it—and you wouldn't, either—if you'd met Mister Numar."

"Harry," broke in Annabelle, "I don't think it's nice for you all the time interrupting Granny when she's telling us this wonderful story."

"There's just one more thing I want to know," said Harry. "What did the Green Man come to earth for?"

Grandma Hopper's bifocals were getting misty again. She took them off and started polishing.

"To deliver a message to the creatures on this planet," she said.

"A *message*," repeated Harry. "*What* message?"

"You're getting ahead of my story," said Grandma Hopper, "and I won't tell you—till the right time comes."

THIS declaration effectively silenced the inquisitive, investigative urge in Harry, the III. He subsided with his ears on the alert.

"Let's see now—where was I?" mused Grandma Hopper, re-collecting herself. "Oh, yes—when I found that Uncle Will and Aunt Nellie's house guest was a man from another planet, I naturally wanted to meet him—and after I had, I still wasn't sure he was genuine—and neither was Aunt Nellie. She told me that Uncle Will's car had broken down the night before as they were descending Mount Wilson from the Observatory and Uncle Will had gone off in search of a telephone to call the garage in the valley. All of a sudden he came back to the car with this strange-appearing Green Man and introduced him to Aunt Nellie as 'Mister Numar, from the Planet Talamaya.' He told Aunt Nellie that he'd just seen Mister Numar arrive by space ship—and that Mister Numar had stopped the motor of the car by some sort of wave so they could meet—and that he, Uncle Will—had been chosen by Mister Numar to be his host or sponsor while he was staying on earth."

Harry and Annabelle were bug-eyed with interest.

"Gee, Granny, I've just got to ask," cried Harry. "Did our Great Great Aunt Nellie see the space ship?"

"No," said Grandma Hopper. "No one but your Great Great Uncle Will ever saw the space ship. Mister Numar said its technical development was so far beyond anything we knew about that it would only confuse and bewilder us to see it—so he had it rendered *invisible*."

Harry's face registered disappointment and disbelief.

"There's something fishy about *that*," he declared. "Go ahead—I'll figure it out later."

"Well," said Grandma Hopper, "Aunt Nellie didn't know what to make of things, but Uncle Will seemed so convinced the Green Man was the real article she had to let him take Mister Numar home—and then her troubles began."

"Troubles!" said Annabelle. "Why, I think it would be wonderful to have a man from another world in your home."

Grandma Hopper reached down to pat the pretty blonde head.

"Not so wonderful on an earth like this," she replied, "where humans don't believe in anything they can't see or hear or taste or touch or smell..."

"But they could see and touch the Green Man, couldn't they?" asked Annabelle. "I thought you said...?"

"Yes—but he wouldn't photograph," said Grandma Hopper. "There was something about his color or the vibrations of his body—no one ever discovered what—but there wasn't a camera that could get his picture. They took movies of me, hugging and kissing the Green Man—and trying to get away from him when I got shocked—but when the films were developed, it looked like I was dancing the rhumba all by myself."

"Have you still got those pictures?" asked Harry.

"I suppose the newsreel companies have them somewhere in their files," said Grandma Hopper. "And I've got some newspaper pictures. But they wouldn't mean anything without the Green Man in them. No one would ever believe he was actually there."

Harry began to look a trifle dazed.

"Gee, Granny—this is the dizziest story I ever heard. It gets nuttier and nuttier, the further you go."

Grandma Hopper nodded. "I know it does—that's the reason I said in the beginning that I hadn't told it to you before—not until I thought you might be old enough."

"Go on," invited Harry. "We're old enough—maybe too old for a fairy tale like this!"

"EVERYTHING was a fairy tale before people accepted it as a fact," reminded Grandma Hopper. "The telephone, the automobile, the airplane—hardly anyone believed they were possible at the start—and they won't believe that the Green Man was actually here on earth until he comes again."

"Comes again!" cried Harry and Annabelle together. "Is he going to do that?"

"I've been expecting him," said Grandma Hopper. "He didn't exactly promise he'd come—but he sort of hinted."

"Do you suppose he'd visit us, if he did?" asked Annabelle, the pupils of her eyes dilated.

"I think he would—just for old times' sake," said Grandma Hopper. "Just think, children—the Green Man was actually in this very house. It's one of the reasons your Great Great Uncle and Aunt left this house to us when they died—because your grandfather and I had shared with them their remarkable experiences with Mister Numar."

"Gee, Granny," said Harry, "you're making this house sound like it's *haunted.*"

"It is," said Grandma Hopper, "with *memories.* My—the crowds of curious humans who came out here to see the Green Man—they ruined Uncle Will's lawn and garden—and when the newspapers announced to the world that Professor William Bailey, eminent astronomer, was entertaining a visitor from Space—well, there was no peace, day or night, after that. All kinds of offers began pouring in from radio shows, Broadway and Hollywood producers, lecture bureaus, state fairs, circuses and the like—for the Green Man to make personal appearances. Most people thought he was a gigantic hoax but they wanted to cash in on him just the same—and I did, too."

"*You,* Granny?" asked Harry, incredibly.

"Yes," confessed Grandma Hopper. "I was young and ambitious—and I could see where my going on tour with the Green Man would give me a lot of publicity and help make my name in Hollywood."

Harry regarded his grandmother, thoughtfully.

"Did you believe in him then?"

"No—not really, I guess. It was all so exciting—and talent scouts from M.G.M. and Warner Brothers were after me—and trying to sign up Mister Numar, too—and he was booked to appear on the 'Frank Morgan' and 'Information, Please' radio programs…"

"What programs were *they?*" asked Annabelle.

"Frank Morgan was one of our funniest comedians then—and 'Information, Please' was a question and answer program—very intellectual—with a committee of experts—men who knew a little something about everything—and they wanted the Green Man to match his intellect with theirs."

"Did he do it?" asked Harry. "How'd it come out?"

"Mister Numar was too kind to show them up," said Grandma Hopper. "He could have read their minds and gotten all the answers. He did it once, just to demonstrate—and recited some Shakespeare. After that, he sat back and let them do the starring."

"Did he get paid, same as they did?" asked the practical Harry.

"Oh, yes—but since his planet of Talamaya didn't have any money system and he didn't need any money here—he just signed his checks over to Uncle Will."

HARRY shook his head. "I can't imagine a planet with people on it and no money," he said. "Must be a funny place."

"I presume every inhabited planet has different customs and practices," said Grandma Hopper. "It would be a pretty dull Universe if they didn't. Well, after Mister Numar appeared on these two radio programs we went with him to Washington where he spoke to a joint session of Congress and we all met the President of the United States."

"Gee," said Harry. "Honest…? You and our Great Great Aunt and Uncle…?"

"Yes—and the two talent scouts from M.G.M. and Warners," said Grandma Hopper. "We made quite a party. And we went from Washington to Chicago where Mister Numar had been invited to deliver his message to the world between halves of a football game at Soldiers' Field."

"My gosh," exclaimed Harry. "Gee whiz, Granny—you sure traveled around."

"And everywhere we went," said Grandma Hopper, "we were met by thousands and thousands of people—newspapers and magazines and radio programs were full of news on every move of the Green Man. The F.B.I. had investigated him and couldn't prove him a fraud. He was the super sensation of the day—and when he stood before a crowd of one hundred and thirty thousand people in Soldiers' Field that afternoon, he had lined up for him the greatest radio network in history—with millions listening in all over the world."

"What did he say?" demanded Harry. "Have you come to his message yet?"

"Yes," smiled Grandma Hopper. "Mister Numar had told us, out in California, that he wanted to deliver his message to the human creatures on our planet from the city of Chicago because Chicago would eventually become the headquarters for the Peace League of All Nations—and he was interested in the future of life on this earth—not its past."

"He wasn't such a good prophet," said Harry. "That hasn't happened yet."

"No—but Chicago's just about become the headquarters for everything else," said Grandma Hopper. "Commerce, aviation—even government—and there's talk of making it the capitol of the United States, which Mister Numar also predicted it would become."

"So what?" cried Harry, impatiently. "Tell us his message! What did the Green Man say?"

Grandma Hopper paused. She knew she had come to the climax of her story and she wanted to make the most of it.

"If you don't believe in the Green Man you won't believe this," she warned.

"We believe," assured Annabelle, eagerly. "Tell us, Granny!"

"I'm not saying whether I believe or not," hedged Harry, the III. "But tell us, anyway."

"WELL," continued Grandma Hopper, "I can almost remember Mister Numar's message word for word it made such a lasting impression on me. He said: 'I, Numar, the Awakener, am here... I have been sent to speak a prophesy to you. A Great Light is soon to appear in the heavens. Its brilliance will startle all mankind. It will cast an illumination over the entire earth. It will mark the beginning of a great change to take place on your planet. It will awaken all humans to the realization that there is a power far greater than themselves...'"

"Wait a minute, Granny," interjected Harry, excitedly. "What year did the Green Man say this?"

"It was back in Nineteen Hundred and Forty-three."

"That's thirty-two years—and no Great Light yet."

"No—but thirty-two years is nothing to a Being who has lived millions," replied Grandma Hopper. "It's not even *yesterday*. Mister Numar went on to say that the presence of this great phenomenon in the heavens would cause the greatest spiritual revival known to man...that awe-struck millions would search their souls as never before...and when this Great Light appeared, a host of Higher Intelligences would arrive sent here to work with our leaders...and that Man would commence to grope from threatened chaos toward a new harmony with all things."

Harry, the III, and Annabelle sat, unspeaking. This was obviously too much for them.

"I can see now," said Grandma Hopper, after a long moment, "that I should have waited until you were older. This is too far over your heads."

"What did the world think of the message?" Harry finally asked.

"Pooh-poohed it, generally," Grandma Hopper admitted, sadly. "Called Mister Numar a new kind of cultist—a clever magician who had fooled everybody—and would now probably try to found a new religion."

"What became of him?"

"He flew back to the coast with us—and your grandfather, who met him there—drove him to the place in the mountains where his space ship was hidden. Then Mister Numar bade us all farewell..." There were sudden tears in Grandma Hopper's eyes. "And I asked him if we'd ever see him again...and he smiled at me and said: 'There's an eternity of time ahead. Perhaps we shall all meet again, somewhere.'"

"How nice," said Annabelle. *"Then* what did he say?"

"He left the road and started off alone, up the mountain side toward his invisible space ship—and turned and waved at us—and said: 'You will think of me when the Great Lights appears.'"

"Did you see him leave?" asked Harry.

"Yes—he had told us to watch over the treetops—and suddenly there was a blinding silver beam of light, which shot up and out of sight so fast our eyes couldn't follow—and he was gone."

"My," exclaimed Annabelle, in awed tones, "that must have been something."

"The most wonderful experience of my life," said Grandma Hopper.

There was another moment of stillness, then, from Harry: "Granny—what's Daddy think of this story?"

"He doesn't know what to think."

"Well, I can tell you what I think," announced Harry, the III. "I think, Granny, you're just plain bats—and, if I were you—I'd see a psychiatrist."

CHAPTER TWO

ELLEN HOPPER was not her mother's daughter as to looks. She resembled her late father, possessing his dark eyes and hair, a certain amount of dash and daring—and a determined chin. An attractive career woman needed that in the National Capitol—or anywhere else, for that matter.

Ellen had done all right by herself, so far, as one of the inner ring of Presidential secretaries. A crack stenographer, she was "in" on important staff meetings and private conferences, being required to make notes or actual recordings of what transpired.

Interested as she was in world events, the position thrilled her. Like having a front seat where history was being made—meeting or seeing the big people of her own and foreign countries—sizing them up at close range, forming her personal opinions of them—some of which would not have looked well on paper.

Ellen kept a diary, however, in which she listed a few of her private impressions of world leaders and personal acquaintances. It would have made interesting reading had any of those mentioned been able to scan her appraisal of them. Ellen's notations had been put down at random and in no certain order.

NORMAN ELLSWORTH—President Rubber stamp

BYRON WOODRUFF—Secretary of State
  Ditto

ANDREW BROWNELL—Assistant Secretary of State
  Bright boy—but where will it get him?

PETROV GOUCHEVISKY—Attaché of Russian Embassy
  If he were only an American!

DEWITT HARVEY—National Party Chairman
  He cracks the whip and the President jumps!

JEFFREY MERRILL—Secretary of Labor
  I'd like him better without spats.

FRANK FAULKNER—Secretary of Agriculture
  All corn—and a mile high!

GENERAL HENRY WADE—Secretary of War
  Who's plugging for a shooting war against Russia

PERCY HAMLIN—Secretary of the Navy
  Why let battleships rust when they can be used?

GENERAL GEORGE CARLTON—Secretary of Aviation
  Why have an Army and Navy?

CORNELIUS VANDERTON—Financial Advisor to the President
  Heaven help the small businessman!

ALVAH PETRIE—Head of the Amalgamated A.F. of L. and the C.I.O.
  The irresistible force.

STANLEY JENSEN—President of National Manufacturers
  The impenetrable object.

MISS KATHERINE BARKER—Andy Brownell's Secretary
  She likes Andy—and *I* hate *her!*

IT CAN be seen from a glimpse at Ellen's diary that she had none too high a regard for most politicians and government officials. At the age of twenty-five, she was worldly wise to the point of disillusionment. When a girl, she had heard her mother tell, as part of a bedtime story, of a visit to Washington in company with a fabled Green Man. Her mother had met on this trip many of the country's outstanding celebrities and there had been born in Ellen, from that moment, the desire to meet and associate with important people.

Now, for the past three years, she had been doing it, which had led her to wonder why she had selected a career in place of romance and a home. But it was by no means too late. Two very likely prospects in the matrimonial department were all but knocking at her door. Ellen had, thus far, not permitted the developing interest to grow too serious. Perhaps it was because she feared any indication of preference might bring about a minor international incident—since an American and a Russian were involved.

Tonight, as her mother had been telling, for the first time to her grandchildren, the fanciful story of old, Ellen was declining an invitation from persuasive, personable Petrov Gouchevisky to take in a neighborhood movie.

"I can't, Pete," she said, over the phone. "Sorry."

"Why not? You haven't anything on for tonight…"

(She loved the Russian accent behind the perfect English he spoke.)

"How do you know that?" she asked.

Petrov's laugh rippled over the wire. "My Dear—the Russian spy system is everywhere."

"All right, then. What am I wearing tonight?" challenged Ellen.

"Something beautiful—a dress of some kind—it's lovely— anything on you looks lovely—especially tonight."

It was Ellen's turn to laugh. "Your Russian spies will have to do better than that. Your phone call got me out of the bath."

There was a pause but not for long. "My spies were still right," insisted Petrov. "They told me you had nothing on for tonight—and you haven't! How about that picture show?"

"No," refused Ellen. "I have an appointment in half an hour. Honest, Pete. Try me again, some time soon."

"But they're running a short on Russia I wanted you to see. Our parachute army. Thousands jumping at one time. Very thrilling."

"All propaganda," denounced Ellen. "Probably one parachute jumper reproduced thousands of times. Some other night, Pete. Have to cut you off now. Bye, bye."

As Ellen hung up she could hear Petrov good-naturedly saying something uncomplimentary in Russian.

AT THE Municipal Airport in Washington, D.C., a special transoceanic State Department's plane was arriving from Europe. On this plane was the other man in Ellen's life, Andrew Brownell, special troubleshooter for Secretary of State Byron Woodruff. He had been on a six weeks' secret mission to Russia, the Far East and returning via Europe and England.

Ellen was proud of Andy. He was just under thirty and rated the most brilliant diplomatic prospect on the country's horizon. That he had reached this position of eminence without family wealth or influence was vastly to his credit and considered by old-line politicians and diplomats a minor miracle.

Andy had graduated at the University of Michigan, majoring in languages and world affairs, and had then gone abroad on scholarships, serving as translator with United States embassies in Moscow, Paris and Buenos Aires. Having acquitted himself well abroad, Andy had been recommended for special assignments and had returned to the States to work directly under Chief Woodruff.

It was Andy's poise, under any and all circumstances, far beyond his years, together with his facile mind, which had given him almost overnight diplomatic standing in the capitols of the world. He was not handsome appearing but there was a direct sincerity in his frank blue eyes and friendly manner. He stood exactly six feet, although his springy chestnut brown hair made him seem taller.

Ellen thus reviewed her estimate of him as she taxied to the airport to be present at his arrival.

"He's certainly different from Petrov," she compared. "That Russian's about the best looking male I've ever seen any time, anywhere. I wonder if all Georgians have that commanding way about them? With those dark eyes and hair and that physique, he could crash Hollywood. He's the glamour boy of foreign diplomats."

The taxi was turning in at the Municipal Airport. There was quite a heavy overcast and wisps of fog hung over the Potomac, but the floodlights were on and Ellen could hear the roar of the six-motored "Cosmic Traveler" as it circled overhead, preparing for the customary instrument landing.

The plane was down and rolling to a stop in front of the Air Terminal. Ellen tossed a bill at the taxi driver and ran through the gateway to join the usual throng of greeters. There would be easily three hundred passengers on this Goliath of the air, representing many celebrities for newsreel men to shoot and reporters to query.

Ellen, pushing through the crowd, felt an elbow in her ribs. A side-glance revealed the owner of the elbow—Andy's overly attentive, always-on-the-job secretary—the hated Katherine Barker.

"Hello, Ellen," she smiled. "Trying to fly to Mr. Brownell? He's coming down, you know. In fact, there's the plane now— right ahead of us."

"Yes, I see it," raged Ellen, inwardly, returning the smile. "Sorry I ran into your elbow. Excuse it, please."

Katherine had green eyes and they looked now, as Ellen thought, green with jealousy.

"You won't be able to see Mr. Brownell tonight," said his secretary, in her irritatingly efficient manner. "He's going to be closeted with Mr. Woodruff."

Ellen put a little ice in her voice. "Perhaps you will make an appointment with him, long enough to permit me to say 'hello?'"

Katherine gave out with a laugh, the texture of peanut brittle. "Oh, of course, if that's all you had in mind. You don't need any appointment for *that*."

THERE was no love lost and none to be found between these two women. From the first time Andy had commenced dating Ellen, the fight was on—open undeclared warfare. Andy had not appeared to be aware of the rivalry. His mind had been too filled with world problems to concern himself over the boundary disputes of two "feminine states." Ellen was certain he had not given Katherine a romantic thought—but Katherine was working on him—trying to make herself indispensable and almost ever present. She didn't mind overtime or night sessions—anything to be in the company of the State Department's white-haired boy.

"What she needs is an overdose of sleeping tablets," thought Ellen. "She's a pain in my neck. But, at least, she lets me know where she stands. Maybe if I were in her place and felt as she does I'd try to build a fence around the man I wanted to make my property, too."

Passengers were disembarking from the airplane's huge underbelly. Flashlight bulbs popped and sputtered. Secretary of State Woodruff and his aides were up front. They would be the first to speak to their returning associate.

Ellen had eyes only for Andy Brownell. No other plane traveler from abroad held any interest. She permitted Julian Neal, Hollywood's latest romantic sensation, to pass unnoticed within a few feet of her, as other women almost swooned for his attentions and begged for his autograph. He was not her type of hero.

"There he is," sighed Katherine, and edged in ahead of Ellen. "You'll pardon me, I'm sure. He'll have some papers and things to give me. I'll tell him you're here."

"Don't bother," said Ellen. "He'll see me. I'll look out for myself, thank you."

Andrew Brownell met a barrage of newsreel floodlights and camera flashes as he stood in the plane's doorway and started to descend the ramp. He was bareheaded, chestnut hair, disheveled as ever, glinting in the changing illumination. His usually genial face was taut and unsmiling as he shook hands with his Chief. Byron Woodruff was stout, pompous and almost pot-bellied. He was scion of the long line of wealthy Woodruffs, the international oil barons. He had been trained for this post, thought Ellen, to help his family protect their multifarious interests in foreign lands. Money was still power— it bought special privileges and position, as of old—and the Woodruffs were said to practically own the Party.

Ellen was not close enough to hear what was being said by the officials greeting Andy. But now the State Department's troubleshooter was being asked to make a statement for the press and the newsreels.

"Sorry," he declined. "There's nothing I can say until I've seen the President."

Police officers were now making a lane for Andrew Brownell and his group to walk through to waiting limousines.

"Let me through, please," requested Katherine. "I'm Mr. Brownell's secretary."

"Certainly, Miss." The officer stepped aside and Miss Barker hurried to Andy's side.

Ellen, behind the lines, saw him hand her his briefcase and say a few words in her ear. She nodded and ran on ahead, toward the cars, flashing a triumphant glance at Ellen as she passed.

But Andrew Brownell, now that the official greetings were over, was obviously looking for someone. He scanned the lane of spectators, stepping out of the glare of spotlights to do so. Then he sighted Ellen—and crossed over to her, extending his hand.

"Hello," he said.

Ellen felt the ground heaving under her feet. Was it her heart pounding or was the earth trembling?

"Have a nice trip?" she heard herself asking.

How foolish and inconsequential. But what could anyone say in a public place like that? Andy was keeping his Chief Woodruff waiting. Katherine, looking back, must be burning.

"Very," Andy was answering, in a low, cautious voice. "I was hoping you'd be here. It may be late—but can I call on you—at your apartment?"

Ellen nodded. "I'll be waiting," she whispered.

Andy released her hand and rejoined his State Department crowd. Ellen saw him get in the limousine with State Secretary Woodruff—alone. The other officials were left to follow in other cars, to one of which Katherine, herself, had been assigned.

"Serves you right, old girl," smiled Ellen. "You *will* try to cut me out, will you?" Then her thoughts sobered. "But, say— something must be up. Andy's never asked to see me at my apartment before—and late at night, too. I wonder…"

IT WAS almost three in the morning, when Ellen, dozing in her bachelor apartment, heard the self-service elevator at her floor, soft footsteps, and then a light tap on the door. She opened it, attired in a cheery yellow housecoat of loose weave material, with contrasting sandals. She made an attractive picture for Andy as he entered, shutting the door quietly behind him and slipping the lock.

"Well," said Ellen, "this is secret diplomacy. Locking a girl in her own apartment at three o'clock in the morning."

Andy turned to look at her. She still hadn't seen him smile.

"It's possible I was followed," he said, after a moment. "That was just in case."

He crossed over to the little table, near her easy chair, and took up a cigarette. She observed him to be under great tension.

"Hot coffee?" she asked.

"Yes," he said, dropping into her chair. "Black and strong— plenty of it."

"I'll have it for you in five minutes," she volunteered, moving toward her kitchenette. "You just lie back—and relax."

The coffee was soon sizzling in the pot. Ellen, eyeing Andy from her position near the gas burner, saw him staring at her blue painted ceiling, emitting nervous puffs of cigarette smoke. This was so unlike him. In all the time she'd known him, he had never outwardly revealed his feelings. She placed the coffeepot on her little tea table and made a noise with the cups and saucers. She fancied she saw Andy start.

"You *are* quick, aren't you?" he said, as she rolled the table in and poured out the coffee, hot, black, strong-smelling.

Ellen smiled. "That's because you've been miles away."

Andy nodded and took a deep draught of the coffee. Then he set the cup down and turned abruptly to Ellen who had seated herself, squaw fashion, on a comfortable floor cushion in front of him.

"Ellen, how much do you care for me?" he asked.

No warning, no soft music, no lights, no romantic approach—just—bang! It caught Ellen as unprepared as a sneak attack. But Andy's maneuver had been deliberate, he was studying her face intently, noting her reaction, awaiting her reply.

"Not quite as much as I had hoped for," he guessed, when there was no answer.

"That's not fair," protested Ellen. "Training your big guns on me, like this, and opening fire. A girl has to have a few seconds to think out a question like that..."

"That's just the trouble," said Andy, grimly. "There's very little time for anything left—for thinking or living or romance. I just thought—if you cared as I care we'd get married later today—and enjoy what happiness we can together before..." He broke off and crushed the cigarette in the ashtray. "Oh, hell. What's the use?"

ELLEN leaned forward and put a hand on his knee.

"Andy, I do care. I care for you very much. I'm not quite sure yet about my loving you enough to…well, today is awfully short notice."

"I know," said America's youngest and most brilliant diplomat. "And there'll always be a tomorrow—but there won't. Time is short—short for everything—all life on this planet. You and I and every human can only be certain, from now on, of our present moment—this very instant. One second from this one, we may be in oblivion."

Ellen regarded Andy with a sudden surge of alarm. She got to her feet, reaching for the coffeepot.

"Another cup? You look like you could use about thirty-six hours' sleep."

"Sleep!" cried Andy. "God, Ellen—if you knew what I know—you couldn't ever sleep again! It can't be averted. It's apt to break out any minute. We're on the verge of another world war!"

Ellen sat herself in a nearby straight chair, still holding the coffeepot. She tried a smile.

"Whew… Andy, you really had me scared… But I've gotten accustomed to the threat of new world wars. We've had that talk in our daily diet for years and years. The Russians were going to attack us as soon as they shared the atomic bomb secret after the Second World War. Well—they got the atomic bomb and proved it to us by blowing a big hole in the Arctic ice fields, which upset weather conditions for two years—but they didn't pick on us. Then they developed rockets, same as we did, which could be shot to the moon—but they didn't load these rockets with atomic bombs and drop them in our front yard. Finally, everyone predicted, when all the countries of Europe became Sovietized, the Russians would jump on us. That's happened, too—and they've still left us alone. We may have been living in two worlds—which isn't exactly healthy—and we may both have been keeping armed to the teeth, to use a corny expression—but why should there be any more reason to believe we're on the brink of a precipice at this particular moment?"

Andy had gotten to his feet and was pacing the small living room.

"You've just presented a beautiful picture, my dear Ellen, of the delightful complacency of the average American. It's taken years to completely drug us—to make us insensible to any thought of possible danger. The Russians have turned on the charm—have conducted themselves in such a way as to cause many of us to say, 'Communism isn't so bad—for those who may prefer it. Of course, Communism is not for us in this country but, since we couldn't keep Europe from going communist and since the Commies have decided to let us alone over here, we've probably been worrying unnecessarily.'"

ELLEN nodded. "I think what you say is true, Andy. But what's so awfully wrong about that? We, in the United States tried to re-make the world after the Second World War—we spent billions and almost went broke ourselves before we discovered that money could not create democracies. Unless we could keep millions of humans fed and happy—unless we could educate them to a new way of life—their empty stomachs would make them join any movement that promised something better. Now what have we got? Unsettled conditions everywhere— almost every country in the world hating us, and we're still trying to mind everyone else's business. Why don't we let the Russians fry in their own stew? If Communism won't work—if it fails everywhere as it seems to be doing—won't that prove to these millions of misguided humans that our form of government—the freedom and opportunities we give our peo- ple—is far better? If we do this maybe Russia herself will change to our way of thinking."

Andy stood, studying Ellen, with a half-angry, half-pitying expression.

"You are a beautiful girl, you have a good mind—and I love you. But you are still extremely naive. Russia knows her communistic system is failing. She knows she is on the verge of a revolution—not the kind of revolution her emissaries have been seeking—but a great and terrible revolt by the wretched humans under her domination. There is only one way this revolt can be crushed and that is sudden, unprovoked attack upon us and our allies. If we can be conquered, then all humans can be subjected to this tyranny and individual freedom, as we have known it, will never more exist on this earth."

Ellen set the coffeepot down. She was thinking of Petrov Gouchevisky—his joking remark that his "Russian spies were everywhere." Petrov was so likeable. Could it be possible that Russia was plotting an assault upon the United States? Was such an offensive as imminent as Andy was suggesting? What information had Andy obtained on his trip abroad, which had so mightily upset him? Perhaps he was close to a nervous breakdown. Perhaps his usually fine, balanced mind had temporarily lost its sensitive powers of analysis and evaluation. This sometimes happened to men who felt their responsibilities too keenly.

"It's hard to believe," said Ellen, after a moment of silence. "I've frankly liked the Russians I've met."

Andy eyed her. "Such as—Petrov?" he asked.

It was point-blank again but, this time, Ellen met the question head-on.

"Yes," she answered, with just a tinge of defiance. "I think he's a fine person."

"So do I," Andy conceded. "I like many Russians individually—but you mustn't forget that they are all a part of the system—and that system is a colossal threat today to the remaining free peoples on this planet."

"But the Russians have to live on this planet, same as we do," protested Ellen. "If they ruin it, by atomic warfare—they ruin it for themselves, as well. What is to be gained by that? Doesn't Man ever learn as simple a lesson as this?"

Andy shook his head several times. "No, he doesn't. The powers that destroy always figure there is going to be plenty left for them in the end. But this time I'm afraid there isn't going to be. That's why I came here to propose—if you really loved me—that we make the best and happiest use of what time is left."

ELLEN looked long and hard at the man she greatly admired. The marriage of Andrew Brownell to a White House secretary would cause a minor sensation in all foreign capitols, to say nothing of Washington, D. C. She knew now, as she checked her feelings of rivalry for Katherine Barker, that she had wanted Andy to propose. But she hadn't wanted romance to come to her at three o'clock in the morning in this melodramatic fashion—and she had no desire to go to her wedding as though running to a three-alarm fire with the fear that the house was going to burn down before one got a chance to live in it. No—Andy had proved most disappointing as a lover. Now—if he had been Petrov, for instance. She could not imagine the Russian—even if "comes the revolution"—not taking time to provide a romantic setting. In fact, he had been building this romantic background by degrees, his technique vastly interesting her. No, as of the moment, Ellen felt a stronger emotional pull in Petrov's direction than in Andy's.

"I think you'll find that this threat of war will blow over," she heard herself saying. "The facts may look alarming and all that—but just think of the great statesmen and other world leaders who've been predicting dire happenings for years. Everyone knows conditions in many lands are frightful but they've been that way for a long, long time despite all we've tried to do about it. Why don't you go to your hotel, Andy, and get a good sleep. Maybe everything will look quite different when you wake up."

Andy nodded. "Perhaps they will," he said. "Perhaps I'm asleep now—and having a nightmare. Perhaps I just dreamed that I was in love with you. Perhaps there's a tomorrow after all. Good night, Ellen...sorry I troubled you."

America's youngest and most brilliant diplomat stepped out the door, and shut it quietly, firmly after him.

Only after he was gone did Ellen get the feeling that she had, somehow, failed Andy in the crisis of his life.

CHAPTER THREE

THE White House secretarial staff was in a stir. Ellen sensed it the moment she reported for work. Something was up that the girls weren't in on—and this was always big news because it seldom happened.

"It's an early morning super super private conference," informed Polly Wiggens, oldest member of the staff. "Every important brass hat in the Army, Navy and Air Corp is closeted with the President. Also all members of the Cabinet."

"What's it about? Anybody know?" asked Ellen.

"Only inkling we can get is that Mr. Brownell is making a secret report on his findings abroad. You can bet your salary that this international situation is plenty serious. They're not permitting any records to be made of what's being said in there—and they won't even allow news reporters in the White House."

Ellen could have kicked herself down Pennsylvania Avenue as far as the Capitol Building. To think of her having had Andrew Brownell, all to herself, in her apartment, earlier this very day—the man high officialdom was listening to this moment—and not having appreciated the opportunity that might have been hers.

Of course, Andy probably would not have talked—but she certainly had offered him little encouragement to confide in her. On the contrary, she had made light of his fears and concerns. But, quite apparently, she was in the minority. Governmental leaders did not turn out in this manner and at this time in the morning unless it was a matter of high urgency.

"Andy must not have slept at all last night," thought Ellen. "He'll really be a wreck when he gets through—and I haven't helped him any."

The session lasted until almost noon and, when it finally broke up, serious faced conferees hurried away, refusing to make comment or see reporters.

Ellen, kept busy with routine Presidential correspondence, felt miserable. As she was about to go out to lunch, her phone rang. If it were only Andy...

"This is the office of Military Intelligence," said a man's voice. "Is this Miss Hopper?"

"Yes," said Ellen.

"Will you come over right away, please? General Monihan wants to see you."

"Right away," promised Ellen, and hung up. You didn't ask questions when you received orders from a Department like that. You just obeyed. But what could the Big Chief want with her?

Met at the door by an orderly, Ellen was ushered immediately into General Monihan's presence. He was a quiet little man, on the balding side, but with boring eyes.

"Sit down, Miss Hopper," he invited, pointing to a straight chair beside his desk. "Smoke?" He proffered her a cigarette from a gold embossed case.

"No, thanks—not now," Ellen declined.

"Suppose you're wondering why I sent for you?" he smiled.

"One always wonders when a person hears from this office," said Ellen.

"I won't keep you long in suspense," said General Monihan. "But, first, I want to pledge you to secrecy on what is discussed here. This is a matter of great importance to our country."

"You can trust me," said Ellen.

"Good. Then we'll come to the point quickly. Just how well do you know Petrov Gouchevisky?"

Ellen started. She felt a tremor go through her. What a question! So unexpected... And how should it be answered?

"Why, I—I don't know just how you mean that, General," she replied cautiously. "I've gone out with Mr. Gouchevisky a number of times—to the theatre, the movies, several dances at nightclubs—"

"You're quite fond of this Russian gentleman, aren't you?" asked the Chief of Military Intelligence.

Ellen's face took on color. "Well, General—I like him—as a friend. He's been very nice to me."

"Is he equally fond of you?"

"Why, I—I believe so—that is—as nearly as I can tell. We seem to enjoy each other," said Ellen.

Her face was on fire now.

"I want you to be completely frank and honest with me," encouraged General Monihan. "You can be sure I would not be asking you these extremely personal questions were there not something of great strategic value involved."

Ellen nodded. "I appreciate that, General."

"As I understand it," the Chief continued, "you are also a good friend of Andrew Brownell's?"

"Yes—I know him."

"You go out with him occasionally?"

"I do."

"You saw him early this morning—in your apartment?"

"Well, I…"

General Monihan smiled. "You did—because we had Mr. Brownell shadowed, for his own protection."

Ellen gestured, helplessly.

"I can't understand, General, the reasons behind this questioning. Have I done anything wrong?"

"No, Miss Hopper. But the fact that you are such a good friend of Andrew Brownell's—and the fact that Petrov Gouchevisky is showing such an interest in you—did this not ever strike you as a bit unusual?"

"No, sir—I can't say that it did."

"KNOWING of the increasingly strained relations between our two countries—can't you see how Petrov Gouchevisky may have considered it good business to play up to a young woman who enjoys, to a certain extent, the confidence of a top man in our State Department?"

"I would not like to believe that," said Ellen, suddenly chilled at the suggestion.

"There are many things, when we are compelled to think realistically, that we would prefer not to believe," pressed General Monihan. "Tell me, Miss Hopper—do you recall this Mr. Gouchevisky ever trying to pump you? To get information from you about government activities—anything at all which might now, as you look back, have seemed suspicious?"

Ellen hesitated, reviewing different occasions in her mind. She shook her head, relieved.

"No, General—I honestly can't recall. He's just seemed interested in having a good time when we're out together. He has a wonderful sense of humor and is quite American in his ways. What's the trouble? Has there been a leak of some military secret? Do you suspect that I may, unconsciously, have passed on some information?"

"Not at all. I only wanted to ascertain Mr. Gouchevisky's attitude when in your company. Apparently he has played his cards extremely well thus far. He's no doubt been building you up for a big pay-off."

Ellen felt a wave of indignation rise up inside her.

"I can't agree with you on that, General. I don't think Petrov's been trying to play smart with me at all. We just like each other, that's all...and it makes no difference to him, who I know."

General Monihan smiled. "I don't wish to hurt your vanity, Miss Hopper, so I won't hammer on that point. But this brings me down to the real purpose of our interview. Mr. Brownell assures me that whatever I deem it wise to reveal is safe with you. In fact, he suggested you for this assignment."

"Assignment?" repeated Ellen, wonderingly.

The Chief of Military Intelligence gazed testily at her.

"Yes, Miss Hopper—we are relying upon you to get much needed information from Petrov Gouchevisky. We have reason to believe that he knows the exact day, hour and minute—even second—that the Russians are going to launch a surprise air and rocket atomic bomb attack upon us."

Ellen sat, frozen in her chair—so ice cold that she couldn't utter a word. It was all too incredible. Petrov liked the Americans—he had many American friends. They all liked him. Why, if he knew that his government was plotting anything like this, Petrov would certainly not help carry it out. It was unthinkable that anyone so big-hearted, so high-spirited...

"This specific information we must have, if it is at all obtainable," Ellen heard General Monihan going on. "Can we count on you to help us get it?"

"I don't know," said Ellen faintly. "What would you want me to do?"

"Very simple," directed the Chief. "Go out with Mr. Gouchevisky...get alone with him, if possible, at a bar or some eating place, wherever he wishes. Then drop some of these 'talk tablets' in his drink. They'll loosen his tongue and he won't be able to withhold the information you want when you commence asking questions."

Ellen moistened her lips, nervously.

"I'm afraid I wouldn't be much good at this sort of thing."

"You're the only one we know of who is in position to get us this knowledge. It can easily mean the saving of your country. If we knew, positively, that Russia was going to attack us on a certain day and hour, we would have no alternative but to attack Russia first."

"But why can't we trust Russia? Don't we expect Russia to trust us?"

"You can't trust a gun in the hands of the wrong party," said General Monihan.

"Isn't it possible Russia feels the same way toward us?" countered Ellen.

"Quite possible," the Chief conceded. "When two great countries have basically different ideologies, this is always the case...it's been true throughout all history."

"Then does this mean there will always be wars? Or possibilities of war?"

"UNTIL one power or the other triumphs—or both go down together," said General Monihan. "Unfortunately, Miss Hopper, this appears to be human nature and no matter how highly advanced civilization becomes—the fight for power continues."

Ellen had an almost overwhelming feeling of revulsion. "I'm commencing to regret that I was ever born on this planet," she said.

"But being born," pursued the Chief of Military Intelligence, "and being an American—you now have a job to do. The information you gain can possibly save the world from being plunged into another Dark Ages. There is obviously no choice between our way of life or the Russians. Individual freedom or individual slavery for all Mankind is the issue. What is your answer?"

Ellen lifted her determined chin.

"The way you put it there can only be one answer," she said, with spirit. "I'll accept the assignment."

General Monihan nodded, gravely. "It is not without certain elements of risk. The Russians can be relied upon to deal severely with any person or persons whom they suspect of trying to get this information. You may not find Petrov Gouchevisky so charming if he realizes you have gained vital knowledge from him."

Ellen stood up. She was highly tense, inwardly, but well controlled outwardly.

"I may as well tell you, General, that I will be astounded if I find that Petrov—I mean, Mr. Gouchevisky, has any information of the kind you seek. It is still unthinkable to me that any great power today, knowing what terrible weapons of destruction each side possesses, should be plotting aggression."

General Monihan arose, extending his hand.

"We will give you such protection as we can, under cover," he said. Then, handing her a small envelope, he added:

"Here are the 'talk tablets.' They are extremely potent. One of them dropped in any liquid drink will have an effect within ten minutes and last for perhaps half an hour. Create the opportunity for such a situation and go to work. Our entire course of action waits upon your report."

Ellen straightened. "I shall try, General, not to fail you—or my country."

The Chief of Military Intelligence smiled.

"I am sure you will," he said.

"One question," asked Ellen. "Shall I wait for Mr. Gouchevisky to contact me—or shall I invent an excuse to see him?"

"Give him a day or so," advised the General. "We have reason to believe he will be getting in touch with you. He has already been informed, by his own agents, that Andrew Brownell spent some time in your apartment this morning."

Ellen reeled as though hit solidly between the eyes. General Monihan had evidently saved this knockout punch for the last. Commingled feelings of rage and humiliation surged within Ellen as she groped her way from the Office of Military Intelligence and walked unsteadily down the corridor, seeking the fresh air.

So Petrov knew of her night meeting with Andy. Then he'd probably known of every other date she'd had with the State Department's star troubleshooter. Not only that—he'd no doubt had a report on her every movement. Ellen quickly reviewed her past actions. Nothing to cause her any real personal embarrassment except this session with Andy in her own apartment at such an hour. How would any other man interpret such an apparent *rendezvous*? What kind of a young woman would he think her to be? And what kind of person was

Petrov Gouchevisky? Had she misjudged him? Did he have a diabolical side to his nature? Was this true of all Russians?

Ellen drew a deep breath of resolution. She intended to have the answer to some of these questions—and soon.

CHAPTER FOUR

THE prediction of the Chief of Military Intelligence was not long in being fulfilled. The following day, Ellen had barely reached her apartment from work than the phone commenced ringing.

"It's I, Petrov," said a familiar voice. "My spies report that you've just arrived home."

"Oh, stop it," cried Ellen. "You and your spies. Keep this up and you'll soon have me looking behind doors and under beds."

Petrov's chuckle filled the receiver.

"Might be a good idea," he said. "Listen, Ellen—I know this is short notice—but I've just secured a new Chinese cook and the dishes he prepares…"

"Russian dishes?"

"No, no—he cooks in any nationality you want. But I thought—instead of going out to a restaurant, why couldn't you come here and dine with me—and I'll have a dinner cooked to your order!"

Ellen hoped Petrov did not hear the involuntary gasp of surprise, which escaped her. She had, of course, never been to his apartment—nor to any man's, for that matter. But Petrov's invitation, whatever his own motives, was certainly well timed for her purposes.

"How thrilling," she accepted. "And how nice of you, Petrov. I'll come. What time do you want me?"

"Well, let's see now," said his voice. "It's a quarter to six. What do you say to eight o'clock?"

"Just fine for me," said Ellen.

"Good. What shall I tell Wu Lung to fix for you?"

"Oh—something he's probably never heard of—just good old American southern fried chicken—and apple pie, a la mode."

Petrov laughed. "All right tonight will be American night. I'll have the same. And if Wu Lung can't fix it—I will!"

The receiver clicked. Petrov had a way of cutting off the conversation without formality. Ellen sat by the phone for a moment as goose pimples seemed to break out from every pore. Tonight was ticketed for high adventure. There were tremendous stakes involved—so tremendous she didn't dare think too much about them. And personal stakes, too—involving a very strong romantic feeling for Petrov, which only increased her danger.

"So Andy recommended me for this assignment," she reflected. "And I haven't heard from him since he left my apartment yesterday morning. Looks like he's thrown me over, as far as personal interest goes—but I don't much blame him. If Russia is really planning to attack us no wonder he can't sleep nights. Or any time. Oh, this is monstrous, if it's true."

Dress for such an occasion as tonight was most important. Ellen knew she must look alluring to the point of irresistibility. This was most certainly playing with emotional fire but the stakes demanded it. If such information as she was being sent after existed, she must not fail to bring it back.

Ellen looked over her assortment of gowns and selected a soft, clinging blue dinner dress, which set off the lines of her figure. The deeply slashed neckline was inviting while the long sleeves held one, so to speak, at arms' length. Petrov had an eye for style as well as figure. He had never seen her in this. She could tell in advance that he would like it. It would be cat playing with mouse—but—who would be the mouse?

"I only hope I'm a match for him," Ellen said to herself, as she placed the envelope of 'talk tablets' in her purse. "If I lose out, I know I'll never have another chance."

SHE combed her black hair in a long, wavy bob and touched the tip of each ear with a scent of perfume, then spent an undue amount of time on make-up. Everything about her appearance had to approach perfection. She noticed that her fingers trembled as she applied the lipstick. She could feel the quiver against her lips. This would never do. Petrov mustn't sense the slightest apprehension on her part.

At last Ellen passed her own critical inspection in the mirror. She knew she looked as attractive and appealing as she ever had. It was a quarter to eight—time to be leaving.

As she took a cab in front of her apartment hotel, it could have been her imagination but she had the feeling she was being followed. A small coupe, parked across the street, pulled away from the curb and swung in after her.

Petrov Gouchevisky lived in the Chevy Chase district in Washington. He had the small penthouse on top of the Cliff Dwellers Mansion. It was fifteen stories high and commanded a spectacular view. Exclusive, secluded—a little fenced-in garden on the roof, as Ellen was to discover.

The door to Petrov's penthouse was opened by a Chinese butler. The Madame would please step this way to the powder room, please. She found herself in a highly incensed room—very atmospheric but nothing Russian about it.

When she emerged, Petrov was waiting for her in the living room, which glowed with a fire in the fireplace.

"Not exactly the season for a fire," said Petrov. "But I've been burning a lot of old papers—and besides, a fire is always so cheerful."

He took Ellen's hand and held it as his eyes caressed her figure.

"Very, very beautiful. More beautiful than I have ever seen you," he complimented. "Almost as beautiful as you were when I phoned you the other day," he added, and laughed when Ellen withdrew her hand and aimed a playful slap at him.

"You have a charming little place here," she said, by way of distracting his attentions. "And from these windows—is there anything you can't see?"

"Yes," teased Petrov. "You—in your bath!"

"But your spies?" twitted Ellen.

"Ah, that is different," said Petrov. "Our spies see *everything!*"

HE LED her to a landscaped terrace where a table had been set for two. From the direction of the kitchen she could smell the unmistakable appetizing aroma of southern fried chicken.

"You Russians are wonderful," she said. "So hospitable. I wish I could educate my stomach to like foreign dishes but I confess to preferring things—*American style.*"

"American men, too?" asked Petrov. They were seated. His magnetic dark eyes had question marks in them.

"Not necessarily," replied Ellen, as her eyes answered his challenge.

"Then shall we toast our two countries in my native vodka?" proposed Petrov. "Russia has made concessions to your American appetite. It is only fair that you compromise when it comes to the drink."

Ellen nodded, smiling. Both raised glasses, touching them across the table in such a manner that they gave forth a musical ring.

"You see," said Petrov, "we have struck a harmonious note between us. That is good. It should be so between all Russians and Americans."

Ellen touched the liquor to her lips and set the glass down.

"Why can't it be?" she asked, pointedly.

Petrov shrugged his shoulders. "Perhaps too much isolation. Our peoples do not mix enough."

"But how can they when your government does not permit free travel—free exchange of visitors?" demanded Ellen. "You Russians can go wherever you like in the United States—do what you like. But Americans, in your country, are not granted the same privileges. How can we, as a people, ever develop any mutual confidence or liking for you Russians on such a basis?"

Petrov's usually genial face took on a sober look. "Frankly," he said, "I do not know." He raised his glance again. "Shall we drink to a better understanding, in any event?"

The glasses tinkled and Ellen coughed. Petrov laughed. "You shouldn't sip it—you should down it—like this!"

"No," smiled Ellen, "that won't make my wish any more fervent. I feel this thing very deeply, Peter. I feel—if our two great countries don't really get together on a more understanding basis soon it may be too late. It's been going on this way now for years. This armed truce can't last much longer. One of these days—"

Petrov's hearty laugh interrupted.

"Ah! Let's get off these unpleasant subjects. Here comes that southern fry you ordered."

The Chinese butler, with quiet, smiling efficiency, was serving.

"Which choice pieces does the Madam prefer, please?"

"The white meat, thank you," said Ellen, and then, as an afterthought, "the wish bone, too—if it is still unbroken."

The Chinese butler appeared a trifle nonplussed.

"Will the Madam point out the wishbone, please?"

Ellen surveyed the platter and gave a little chirp of delight. "There it is." She indicated with her fork.

"It shall be as the Madam desires," said the butler, and deftly delivered the wishbone to her plate.

Petrov watched this little maneuver with vast amusement.

"You Americans—and your quaint customs," he remarked. "You are fascinated by isms and superstitions—wishing wells—and wishbones."

ELLEN laughed. "Oh, I don't think most Americans actually believe too strongly in all this business…we're interested more as a game. But it's fun to wish on a wishbone. And when we've finished eating let's do it!"

The boyish side of Petrov, of which Ellen was so fond, came to the surface. "Let's," he said, with full enthusiasm.

They ate silently for a few moments, smacked their lips and grinned at one another.

"The best way to eat this chicken is to take it up in your fingers, like this," said Ellen, demonstrating.

Petrov brandished a drumstick, then set his even white teeth in it.

"Very primitive," he said. "That's what makes you Americans so charming. Such delightful lack of culture."

Ellen made an impish face at him.

"This is perfectly proper. A woman by the name of Emily Post approved of this practice years ago."

Petrov laughed. "That woman will probably live longer in memory than most of your Presidents. You Americans follow your customs more religiously than you do most of your laws."

Ellen nodded. "Yes, I guess you're right. I'd never thought of it that way before. It's a part of our free spirit. We rebel against laws, which compel, but when it comes to customs—which we can practice or not of our own free will—well, because the other fellow's doing it we do it."

Petrov's face wore the expression of a man trying extremely hard to comprehend.

"In our country," he said, "laws are to be obeyed—but custom or tradition—why should we practice what may have been outmoded or ridiculous in the first place?"

"Such as *religion?*" asked Ellen.

"Sectarian religion, yes," said Petrov feelingly. "I will answer that question for myself. It's time men of all different races and beliefs stopped talking authoritatively for God—and let God speak to Man. The real one and only God in this Universe can't speak through only one Church. No one group of humans can have a monopoly on God. God is too big—He is everywhere—in all things—in you—in me!"

"Oh, then you really believe in God?" asked Ellen, leaning elbows on the table and putting down the wishbone, which she had stripped clean.

"Of course I believe in God—but not the God of the churches," said Petrov. "He's a man-made God. In His name the worst atrocities in all history have been committed. When it comes to dictatorships, the Church is just as guilty as the world tyrants. Are you going to accuse God—the Intelligence behind this tremendous universe—of Intolerance and Persecution and Bigotry? I know what most of you Americans say of us Russians. We are infidels—heathens—atheists. Barbarians. That is true—of many of us—if it comes to accepting the kind of God you Americans so unthinkingly worship. But I have said enough. I have already risked our friendship by speaking out as I have."

PETROV wiped his mouth with a napkin and crumpled it in his strong hand. His dark eyes were alive with a burning passion. Ellen had never seen him in this mood. She felt awed and a little frightened.

"I admire you very much for telling me just how you feel— just how you think," she said. "That takes courage few human possess—even in this supposedly free country."

"Thank you," said Petrov. "And now—to be sure we preserve our friendship, shall we turn to lighter, less controversial subjects?"

He was smiling again—that contagious, likable grin. Ellen picked up her wishbone.

"Will you wish with me?" she requested. "Just take hold of this end—and I'll hold on right here—and we'll pull. But first, we must each wish for something we want very, very much— and keep it in mind. Are you ready?"

Petrov, gripping his end of the wishbone, nodded, as their eyes met. "Ready," he said.

They each exerted an increasing pressure.

The wishbone resisted, momentarily, then snapped with a sharp crack.

Petrov examined the short end, which he still held.

"So—I have lost my wish," he said, in a strangely sober tone.

"Yes," agreed Ellen. "You lost... I won—but I suppose my wish was foolish—that it can never come true."

"What did you wish?" Petrov asked. Ellen raised her eyes, daringly, to his.

"That you were an American citizen," she said.

They looked at one another for a pulsating instant, then Petrov glanced away, plainly disturbed.

"What was *your* wish?" asked Ellen. Petrov's dark eyes came back to hers and held them, as he said: "That I could take you with me to Russia—as *my wife.*"

A shock, electrical in its intensity, passed through Ellen. The dinner had been completed and the dishes quietly, unobtrusively removed. They were seated alone—and now Ellen suddenly realized that they were perhaps alone in the penthouse. The Chinese servants had stacked the dishes and left, by pre-arrangement. They would no doubt be back later, to finish up, but this was to be a time of absolute privacy for Petrov and herself.

Instinctively, Ellen found herself on her feet and walking out onto the roof garden. She knew that Petrov had arisen also and was following her. What could she say to him? How could she ever go through with her assignment? Drug him into talking freely about his country's possible secret plans when he had just offered her his heart?

Then another explosive question bombed its way into Ellen's consciousness. What if Petrov's proposal were part of a cleverly conceived romantic scheme to break down her resistance—a deliberate play upon her emotions, designed to bring her mind under his influence, prejudice her in his favor, against her own country, her own personal feelings and inclinations?

SHE stood with her back to Petrov, gazing out over the Chevy Chase section of Washington. Suddenly she felt his arms around her and her head pressed back against his shoulder. In the next instant his lips were upon hers and she was in his embrace. Ellen yielded, at first, but as he continued to hold her, she struggled and forced them apart.

"You love me," Petrov was saying to her. "I know all about this Brownell—but you love me! You are going back to Russia. You will live like a queen there. I will make you very happy."

He caught her arms, pulled her to him and kissed her again, full on the lips; then hugged her close and stroked her soft, wavy hair.

"Just say the word, Ellen—you know it's what you want in your heart. Don't worry your head about my being an American citizen. Love laughs at barriers—it's an old, true saying. I am returning to Russia next week. There will be room for you on that plane."

Ellen had not yet found her voice. She was in a whirl of emotions, conflicts and contradictions.

"Pete—please—give me a chance to breathe—to think," she pleaded.

He released her and she walked back through the garden to the little table they had left. Trying to re-collect her senses and mindful of her increasingly distasteful assignment, Ellen turned to Petrov: "Isn't it customary to have an after dinner cup of coffee?" she asked.

Petrov smiled and bowed. "It is awaiting us in the kitchen. Be seated, my lady, and I will bring it."

Ellen sank down in her chair, opening her purse to see about her make-up. Her fingers came in contact with the envelope containing the 'talk tablets.' She would have to manage to slip two of them in his cup of coffee. Concealing them in the palm of one hand, she began to apply her lipstick, repairing the damage done by Petrov's lips. She felt a strong physical pull in his direction—stronger than she wished to admit to herself. If there only weren't such world questions involved... Could they ever to be surmounted? Was she insane, even entertaining a romantic idea with Petrov for one instant? What about Andy? He wasn't so impetuous, so maddeningly overwhelming…but he had great qualities. Perhaps, in more normal times, released from strain, he might prove more sexually appealing. Ellen knew now it would not be enough for her to admire a man because of his fine intellect or position in life…she would have to feel this inner excitement, which Petrov induced in her. That combined with an appreciation of the man's real worth…a love of his personality…the man himself.

Petrov was standing beside her, taking a steaming cup of coffee off a tray, setting his own cup down across from her.

"What—no cream?" asked Ellen, smiling up at him.

"You don't like it black?"

"No—I much prefer a dash of cream."

"Then you shall have it," bowed Petrov. "Anything my lady wishes."

He turned, imitating the movements of a perfect butler, and went into the kitchen.

Quickly, Ellen reached over and dropped the two 'talk tablets' in Petrov's cup of coffee. Her heart was pounding so it seemed that she could hear it.

Petrov was back in the next moment with a little pitcher of cream.

"Say 'when,'" he instructed, as he poured.

"'When,'" cried Ellen, with the black coffee turning brown.

Petrov took his seat opposite her and lifted his coffee cup.

"What will we toast this time?" he smiled.

"Must we toast anything?" asked Ellen, fingering the handle of her cup and watching Petrov intently.

"We toast with everything we drink in Russia," said Petrov. "How about 'to our life together?'"

Ellen set her cup down. "No," she said, impulsively. "I can't give you my answer yet, Peter. It isn't that I don't care for you…very much…but I…"

"All right, then…'to our love,'" proposed Petrov.

THEY lifted their cups—but their touch, this time, produced a hollow, dull sound—quite disillusioning and unromantic. Yet they drank—both eyeing each other soberly—Petrov taking long swallows. He made a slightly wry face.

"Sorry. Guess it stood a bit too long," he apologized.

Ellen nodded. "Not bad, though. I've tasted much worse."

She drank again and watched him empty his cup. Now to play for time until she could observe that the 'talk tablets' were taking effect. She glanced at her wristwatch. General Monihan had said, "in about ten minutes." She would then have half an hour to learn what she could from the man who was close to the Number One Romance in her life.

"Shall we go in the house?" Petrov invited. "It gets a bit cool here in the evening."

She arose as he opened the door and switched off the terrace lights. The fire in the fireplace had burned low, leaving a bank of red embers. Petrov turned on a floor lamp near the divan and motioned to her. She seated herself, deliberately, at the far end, sensing his amorous intentions.

"Not now, Pete. Let's be sensible. Let's talk this thing out," she appealed.

For the first time, Petrov displayed a trace of irritability.

"Love can't be talked out—it's either something you feel—or you don't."

"But falling in love isn't as easy as that today—between two people from opposite sides of the world," said Ellen. "When I marry, I want it to be for keeps. I want to be as sure of happiness as possible before I—"

"Who can be sure of anything today?" Petrov burst out. "Even tomorrow...next week...?"

Ellen looked at him, queerly.

"Strange, you should make a comment like that," she said. "You sounded then just like Andy Brownell."

"I *did?*" Petrov's eyes sharpened. "Is that what *he* thinks— that there may not be a tomorrow?"

Ellen hesitated. Should she repeat what Andy had said to her? She was foolish to have even brought his name up. Well, why not tell Petrov since he'd expressed practically the same thought?

"Yes," Ellen heard herself saying. "Andy thinks this world is about finished. He's very pessimistic about the future."

Petrov got up, crossed over and secured a cigarette. He offered one to Ellen. She took it, placed it between her lips and let him light it. As both emitted puffs of smoke, he remained standing, looking down at her.

"So—your other boyfriend feels that war between Russia and the United States may break out tomorrow?" shot Petrov.

"I didn't say that," rejoined Ellen, startled. "And I don't know what you mean by 'my other boyfriend?'"

Petrov fingered his wristwatch. "Let's stop shadow-boxing, Ellen—what else would you call a man who is permitted to visit you at three o'clock in the morning—in your apartment?"

"I was afraid you'd bring that up," cried Ellen, and bit her lips.

"Why were you afraid?" Petrov followed up. "Did you know that I knew?"

Ellen's mind turned cartwheels. She had blundered badly at the very start. How to get out of this? She covered with a not too convincing smile.

"Didn't you say your spies were everywhere? I thought they'd probably report such an event as this."

Petrov threw his cigarette savagely in the fireplace. The embers flared up and devoured it.

"All right—someone told you that I knew. I'm not questioning what went on in your apartment. Your private life is your private life."

"I don't think it is," challenged Ellen, "if you have really been getting reports on my doings. I wouldn't have believed that, Peter, if you hadn't…"

"ELLEN—you must know—the life of anyone in the diplomatic service can't be private. He's watched constantly. Everyone he associates with or speaks to is also watched. But things are going to change soon—that's why I want to take you back to Russia with me."

Ellen looked at her wristwatch. Ten minutes were more than up. She should begin asking lead questions.

"Meaning you think I would be much safer there?" she queried, pointedly.

Petrov was slow in answering, as though struggling within himself. Then he sat down on the divan beside her and lowered his voice, as though afraid that some invisible ears might hear.

"Yes—if you must know the truth—much safer," he said.

"Meaning that Russia has at last decided to attack us?" Ellen asked, and held her breath, awaiting his answer.

Petrov rubbed a hand across his eyes and pressed fingers against his lips. He was like a man under light hypnosis, reacting to a suggestion or a command.

"You've guessed it," he said.

Ellen's pent-up breath came out with a rush and she gasped for more air.

"How—how soon is the attack coming?" was her next question.

Little drops of perspiration were commencing to stand out on Petrov's forehead.

"I'm burning all private papers now," he confessed, pointing to the fireplace. "The members of our Embassy are packing up. We've been secretly recalled to Russia. We'll be en route, by air, when the first atomic bombs strike."

Ellen bit her tongue to keep from screaming.

"You said you were leaving some time next week?"

Petrov nodded. "Next Wednesday night."

"That's less than five days," computed Ellen, with mounting horror.

"In five days," said Petrov, "this cozy little penthouse will be no more. Washington, D.C., the capitol of your United States of America will be nothing but an ugly hole in the ground. Half of your country will be in ruins."

"Don't say that," cried Ellen, getting to her feet. Then, steeling herself, "Yes, yes—you must tell me—go on. I've got to know—everything—everything! Just what is the time of this attack?"

Petrov paced, animal-like, across the room pounding his forehead with the palm of his left hand.

"I shouldn't tell you...I'm sworn to absolute secrecy...but I love you, Ellen...I must convince you to come with me... The attack is scheduled for one minute after four your time next Thursday morning."

"One minute after four," repeated Ellen. "Next Thursday. Then that gives us only a short time to attack you first."

"What's that? What are you saying?" Petrov demanded.

"I don't know—what did I say?"

"You said it gave you only a short time to attack us first!"

"Did I?" asked Ellen, placing a hand to her head. "Oh, no— I couldn't—I only *thought* it."

"You said it," declared Petrov, now greatly concerned. He crossed to her, took hold of her shoulders and shook her. "Look at me—Ellen Hopper! Tell me the truth! Were you sent here to get information from me?"

"NO, NO—of course not," said Ellen. Then, surrendering to a strange, uncontrollable urge, "I'm lying, Petrov—yes—I was given the assignment to find out what I could. I didn't want to do it—but I'm glad now that I did. This war's got to be averted. I don't know how—but it's got to be!"

Petrov shook his head. "It's beyond all human prevention. I shouldn't have told you. I've violated sacred confidence— betrayed my country—"

"You couldn't help yourself," said Ellen. "I placed 'talk tablets' in your coffee."

Petrov stared at her, unbelievingly, then gave voice to an ironic laugh.

"And I did the same with yours," he confessed.

"You did?" exclaimed Ellen.

They both looked at each other, laughing nervously, feeling the strain.

"Well, at least we know each other's intentions," Ellen said, after an uneasy moment. "Where do we go from here?"

Petrov's face had become a mask.

"We are not going anywhere," he said, in clipped tones. "We have both failed our respective countries—and it will not be safe for either one of us to leave this room. We must die together."

Ellen eyed this man with whom, a few moments ago, she had felt herself to be in love.

"You're joking, of course."

Petrov crossed to his writing desk, slid open a drawer and withdrew a revolver.

"Yes—it is to be a cruel joke on both of us," he said. "In a different world, we might have lived and loved. But honor is still of more value than life. If you leave this room alive, you will most certainly give out the information you obtained from me—and my country will be attacked at once. It is pretty generally agreed that the attacker in the next war will be the victor. What you have told me proves that, if we do not attack the United States, as planned, we ourselves will soon be attacked. It is the old law of survival. I would be a despicable traitor if I did not do everything to protect my country—and you would be likewise—if you failed to stand up for your native land. I respect your position as I hope you respect mine. We are unfortunately caught on the wheels of fate."

Petrov cocked the revolver as Ellen stood facing him, cheeks flushed, eyes distended.

"I have never before killed a human," he said. "I pray forgiveness to the God of the universe for this. I may tell you now that I think both our systems of government have great wrongs in them. But we each are determined to remake the other and not to correct our own wrongs. You, who I believe might have loved me—wanted to make me an American citizen—and I wanted to make you a Russian. So, you see, we are not much better than the systems we are sworn to uphold." He looked down at the revolver and then at the enticing white-lipped figure of Ellen in front of him. "Is there anything you wish to say?"

ELLEN'S mind was clearing. She must outwit the now coldly calculating Petrov if it were humanly possible. The whole future of life on this planet might depend on what transpired in this little room in the next few seconds.

"Yes," said Ellen. "I know this may sound melodramatic, Peter—but if I must die—I wish to die in your arms. I agree, if conditions had been different, we might have loved...I'd like to forget now that we are anything else but lovers...so, if you'll take me..."

Ellen took a step forward, Petrov opened his arms, and she slid into a close embrace, lips upturned.

They kissed—and she felt cold steel against her side, under the heart. But, only for an instant because Ellen suddenly squirmed with the ferocity of a tigress, grasped the astounded Petrov's wrist with both hands and pointed the revolver skyward as a bullet crashed through the ceiling. By exerting leverage, Ellen got Petrov's hand to her mouth and sunk her teeth in it. He dropped the revolver to the floor, cursing in Russian. She pounced on it, made a half turn and flung it through the window. Glass showered down as the revolver, turning end over end, fell fifteen stories to the street.

Petrov had now grasped her by the hair, forcing her to her knees. His fingers closed around her throat.

Down on the street level a siren started sounding. There were footsteps in the hall outside—fists hammering on the door.

Ellen's breath was cut off. It seemed that Petrov's grip would break her neck.

"I've got to kill you—got to!" he was sobbing, in wild desperation.

Ellen went limp and slumped to the floor. As she did so, the door was burst off its hinges and two plainclothes men from the office of Military Intelligence charged in, guns leveled.

"What goes on in here?" one of them demanded, covering Petrov. "Stick 'em up, you!"

Ellen got shakily to her feet, hand to her throat.

"We—we had a little argument," she said. "My, am I glad you men came. Lock this Mr. Gouchevisky up at once. Don't let him communicate with anyone. Not anyone, understand... I'll go right along with you to make certain that he doesn't. And then get me to General Monihan right away. It's very, very important."

The second officer grinned. "Okay, Miss Hopper. We'll take care of this Russian, don't you worry."

Petrov smiled and bowed. "I made a very sad mistake," he said. "It is inexcusable. I underestimated you."

He turned and went out the door, arms raised, guns at his back.

"Watch out he doesn't try to kill himself," warned Ellen. "Don't hurt him. I want him taken in alive."

A curious, excited crowd had gathered on the street but the police had it well in hand. There was a patrol car waiting, from the F.B.I. Petrov was pushed inside.

"Leave some officers in this man's apartment," directed Ellen. "Don't let anything be touched. And give me plenty of police protection until you get me to General Monihan. I'm not afraid for myself—but I *am* afraid for our country."

CHAPTER FIVE

TO ELLEN'S surprise, she found General Monihan awaiting her in his office. With him was the State Department's famous troubleshooter—Andrew Brownell.

"Well," she said to Andy, with a grim smile. "Fancy meeting you here." Andy returned the smile, equally grim.

"I'm glad you're safe. I hope you secured the information we've been after."

General Monihan offered Ellen a chair and she sank into it, suddenly realizing how nerve-exhausted she was.

"I have it," she said. "You were right, Andy. You, too, General. Russia *is* planning to attack. The hour is set for next Thursday morning at one minute after four, Washington time."

The Chief of Military Intelligence and Andrew Brownell exchanged significant glances. Both men then looked at a calendar on the wall and General Monihan picked up the phone.

"Operator—call an immediate conference of the War Emergency Council to take place in the office of the War Department. Top secret. Everyone there on the double-quick!"

Ellen looked curiously at the General and Andy.

"How did you men chance to be here tonight?" she asked. "I didn't inform you that I was going to see Petrov…"

"No," said the Chief of Military Intelligence. "That was one slight mistake you made. But you will recall, I told you we'd give you all the protection we could, under cover. Our men trailed you to his apartment, then notified me that you were at work and stood by to come to your aid, if needed. Apparently they were."

Ellen nodded. "I wouldn't be here if they hadn't arrived when they did." She turned on Andy, who was seated, one leg dangling over the side of General Monihan's large desk, looking down at her, admiringly. "I understand, Mr. Brownell that I have you to thank for what I've gone through tonight."

Andy smiled. "I'm afraid you have. But you were the only one who could possibly get to Petrov—and I think you'll agree now that such information as you have secured was imperative for our country's safety."

Ellen shook her head. "I don't know. It seems hopeless either way. No matter who attacks first—aren't we both apt to be destroyed?"

"That is true," said General Monihan. "But the slight chance of survival rests with the aggressor. If we can hit Russia first—a sufficiently damaging blow—she may be so crippled that we, ourselves, can escape complete destruction. This is our only hope."

Ellen covered her face with her hands. "Oh, it's too horrible to contemplate. Why do I have to be alive at a time like this? Why couldn't I have lived in an age when the world was at peace—before Man became too highly civilized for his own good?"

Andy placed a sympathetic hand on her shoulder.

"I wouldn't know what Age you might have lived in, Ellen, when the world was really at peace. Man has always warred against his fellow man. Maybe the mistake humans made was in thinking they were more than animals...maybe that's the Great Delusion. It's much easier to figure things out if we look upon ourselves as just super animals, inventing more and more fiendish and destructive weapons to kill each other off with. Animals without a soul, without a conscience, without a God..."

"Andy," cried Ellen. "Don't talk that way. You don't believe that and you know it. We're animals just because we *prefer* to be, not because we *have* to be. We're not using our God-given powers. If we started calling on the best within us, right now, there couldn't be any war. Russia wouldn't attack us—and we wouldn't attack her!"

GENERAL MONIHAN broke in on Ellen. "I'm sorry, Miss Hopper. This is no time for philosophizing. It's a time for action. Andrew and I will have to be getting over to the War Department. But, first, I want to ask you a few questions. Do you think Mr. Gouchevisky realizes he was drugged?"

"He not only realizes it," said Ellen, "but he drugged me. We both talked to each other freely. I didn't know why—but I had to answer every question Petrov asked me, too. That's why he tried to kill me—and intended to kill himself. He was determined the information we both had should die with us."

The Chief of Military Intelligence beat a tattoo with his fingers on the desk.

"And we can't hold him incommunicado very long, either. We'll have to respect the immunity granted foreign diplomats. No doubt word has reached Russian Ambassador Mitoff and he is probably, even now, demanding Gouchevisky's release. What do you recall telling him?"

"Not much—because I, fortunately, didn't know much. I told him that Andy had returned from abroad, fearing a surprise attack by Russia and, since I had gotten him to tell me the time of this attack—I said this gave us a very short time to attack first."

General Monihan stood up. "It's perfectly clear, Andrew, that the instant Gouchevisky is able to pass this information on to his superiors Russia will move up her time schedule. She may strike against us at once."

"Quite likely," said the State Department's smartest young diplomat. "Isn't there some charge he can be held on—such as assault upon Ellen with intent to kill—a lover's quarrel? Use that as a smoke screen to keep him?"

"He'll still have the right to see his lawyer," reminded General Monihan, "and the first contact he makes will be all that's necessary."

"I know it would be extremely dangerous for Petrov to see or talk to any of his people," said Ellen. "And I don't have to be told that my own life is in danger. Of course, if we're all annihilated in the next few days, I don't suppose it makes too much difference."

"That's defeatist thinking," said General Monihan. "We've got to do our utmost to protect ourselves right up to the finish—come what may. You'd better go home now, Miss Hopper. You've done your job—and done it magnificently. We'll see to it that your place is well guarded."

"Thank you, General," said Ellen, getting up. "I'm all over my worrying. I've passed on the information. But I would like to know—is Petrov apt to be released soon?"

The Chief of Military Intelligence nodded.

"We might hold him on some pretext for awhile but we'd have to let some of his associates see him—so we might as well let him out. Why? Are you afraid of him?"

ELLEN hesitated. "I really don't know. I don't believe he'd want to hurt me, personally—but if he felt it was his duty—if my being put out of the way would be a service to his country—"

"So you've come to that conclusion at last?" pointed Andy. "You see plainly, now, that this system, of which Petrov is a part, lets nothing stand in the way of its purpose—that you cannot count on a man's fineness of character. He must obey his master—the State!"

Ellen gave a little, half-mocking curtsy.

"I have learned my lesson, Mr. Instructor—the hard way."

"Come on," said Andy, taking her arm. "I'll get you a cab and ride home with you. Meet you in twenty minutes, General—at the War Department."

General Monihan switched out his desk lamp, removed some cigars from a drawer, put them in his vest pocket and started to the door with them.

"Might as well have one last good smoke before they start blowing this world to hell," he said. "Good night, Miss Hopper—sleep tight."

CHAPTER SIX

IN THE cab with Andy, Ellen leaned a throbbing head against his shoulder. He slipped a supporting arm about her.

"I guess I'm as tired tonight as you were when you came to my apartment two nights ago," said Ellen. "I'm sorry about that occasion, Andy. I wasn't very understanding or considerate. But now I can comprehend the enormous strain you've been under—because it's hit me, too."

"Unhappily, it grows worse instead of better," said Andy. "Humans with any feelings of decency left in them, weren't made for such strains. Few can face the awful reality of this moment and retain their sanity. I was trying to run away from it when I proposed to you that we get married and snatch such fleeting happiness as we could. If I renewed this proposal tonight, would you have the same answer?"

"I'm afraid I would," said Ellen. "I'm in a terrible turmoil inside…it seems, right this minute, that all romance has been killed…forever. I've been trying to hate Petrov…and I can't. I'm sure I hate the system he stands for…just as he apparently hates ours. But how can I say that he is less sincere than I am? If I had been brought up in India, would I have Christian convictions? How are we ever going to reconcile different beliefs and points of view? Won't we die for what we believe in just as zealously as those who oppose us? What's the answer, Andy? There's got to be an answer some time, or no answer, no world."

"If I had the answer, I wouldn't be a diplomat," said Andy, "I'd be a world savior."

Ellen sat upright in the cab.

"You know, Andy, that reminds me of something I haven't thought of since I was a little girl. Mother used to say that some day, when things got so bad in this world something was going to happen. A Great Light would appear in the sky—and God-like humans would arrive here to help guide floundering Man out of his self-made chaos."

Andy laughed, hollowly. "They'd better hurry," he said. "Or it will be too late."

The cab had reached Ellen's address. Another car pulled up behind it, containing plainclothes men, assigned to watch over her. One of the men approached Andy as he helped Ellen from the taxi.

"I'm going with you, Mr. Brownell," he announced. "The Chief's taking no chances."

Ellen pressed Andy's arm. "Do take care of yourself, Andy. I just got a flash then. I don't believe I could stand it in this world without you."

The State Department's bright young man whirled about, caught Ellen in his arms—and kissed her.

"Say, Buck," grinned one of the plainclothes men, "just what are we supposed to protect her against?"

Ellen ran quickly into her apartment hotel and Andy reentered the cab, followed by his bodyguard.

"Swell looking dame," he said, admiringly. "Plenty of guts, too."

"She'll need 'em," said Andy. "We all will from now on. War Department, driver—and get me there in a hurry."

IN THE entire history of the United States of America, going back to the days of the founding of the Republic, there had never been a meeting of the country's executives so fraught with fearsome possibilities for the nation's future. Never had men, charged with responsibility for the country's security and protection, been faced with more difficult decisions as to the course of action that should be taken. Never was there more imperative need for clear thinking, uninfluenced by fear or prejudice.

"We would not be in this extreme peril today," declared hotheaded General Henry Wade, Secretary of War, "if we had acted on my recommendations. I've been contending, for years, as you gentlemen know, that we should have attacked Russia and wiped out her threat to civilization before she destroyed us. Now it may be too late."

"It is not too late if our Commander-in-Chief and our Congress give us the green light for an immediate aerial bombardment," said General George Carlton, Secretary of Aviation.

"How can this be done quickly enough?" demanded Secretary of State Woodruff. "We're holding Petrov Gouchevisky in confinement now against the vigorous protests of Russian Ambassador Mitoff and, by morning, there will be a strong warning from the Russian government. Who knows—perhaps even the arrival of atomic bombs? We're on the very rim of an inferno—and the instant the Russians learn that their secret plan of attack is known by us they have only to touch off the volcano."

"All the more reason why we must decide what to do and do it before Gouchevisky is released or permitted audience with any of his associates," emphasized Secretary of the Navy Hamlin.

"The President recognizes Andrew Brownell," said the presiding Commander-in-Chief.

The State Department's troubleshooter, youngest man in the crowded office of the Secretary of War, stood up and surveyed the assemblage of sober-faced executives.

"Gentlemen," he said, "our present feeling of almost complete inadequacy to face this most critical situation in all world history stems, ironically enough, from our Constitution. No more wonderful document was ever drawn up by free men who sought to preserve that freedom for all other men, for all time as citizens of our United States of America. But consider now, with the world as it is organized, how our Constitution binds us in an emergency.

"Confronted with the absolute knowledge that Russia intends to attack us at a certain time, our President must go before both houses of Congress and ask for a Declaration of War.

"While this action is being taken—our enemy can have attacked us!

"Thus, as things now stand, in our form of representative government, a dictatorship like Russia holds all the cards in the ruthless game of war.

"Democracy has all the best of it in peace—and all the worst of it in time of conflict. Warfare, as developed today, moves too fast for legislative bodies. If a man has a club upraised, ready to hit you, there is no time for you to have laws passed, permitting you to defend yourself or strike him first. This is the predicament we find ourselves in this very moment—a predicament our far-sighted statesmen, if any there be, should long ago have circumvented.

"It should be obvious to even a child's intellect that a centralized command, which does not have to gain the consent of the people to attack has, at all times, a colossal advantage over the military of any other country not similarly equipped to act.

"This is Russia's enormous advantage now. One order, issued as I am speaking, can unloose destruction upon us. We will still be debating, in the halls of Congress, our possible course of action when that destruction arrives!"

THE Assistant to the Secretary of State sat down amid a profound silence. Finally a throat was cleared and the President of the United States, looking directly at Andrew, asked: "What do you propose, Mr. Brownell, as the possible solution of our dilemma?"

Andy rose slowly, thoughtfully, to his feet, conscious that all eyes were upon him.

"It is much easier to point out a weakness, Mr. President, than it is to produce a cure," he said. "I haven't the slightest doubt, if this constitutional check had not been provided that our military strategists would have had us in a war with Russia years ago. Our Secretary of War, for one, has made no secret of his conviction that the time to have curbed Russia's diabolical scheme for world aggression was in the beginning of her expansion period, after the Second World War.

"Russia was out to take diplomatic and actual advantage of the economic unrest, the starvation, the political and religious chaos then existing—and to communize all peoples and countries she could. She was eminently successful, thanks to our poor leadership, political blundering, indifference, greed, and stupid belief that money alone could set up democracies.

"We still haven't learned that the man with an axe to grind, whether that axe is worthy or not, will cut ten times as deeply as the man who grinds no axe at all. So Russia has ground away with the axe of Communism until she has all but cut our feet out from under us.

"The question is—could we have stopped Russia and the growth of Communism had we attacked her years ago? Personally, I doubt it. We might have driven it underground, but Communism—like some germs—thrives on adversity and opposition.

"My concern then is not in our omissions or commissions of the past—but our crisis of the present.

"As I see it, we have one of two alternatives. Take the government of our country in our own hands and order an immediate surprise attack upon Russia. Then go before Congress in the morning, confess to our violation of the Constitution, present the indisputable evidence as to why this was necessary, and call upon Congress to pass a retroactive law, granting us permission to have so acted, following up with a Declaration of War."

The State Department's smart young diplomat paused, dramatically, to let this suggestion register. There was a murmur of excited comment.

"Or," he added, "the other alternative, which involves more risk but which respects our Constitution—is for us to dispatch, at once, a strongly worded diplomatic protest to Russia stating that we are aware of her planned attack upon us and that we will attack her within twenty-four hours of this dispatch if we do not receive satisfactory assurances and proof from her that she has abandoned her aggressive intention."

A burst of applause greeted this second suggestion. Andy resumed his seat.

Secretary of State Woodruff addressed the chair. "Mr. President, I am in favor of Mr. Brownell's latter recommendation—even with the added risk involved. Unannounced warfare, on our part, while no doubt a greater protection, lays us open to the horrific reprisals, which are sure to come. While there is yet the remotest chance of averting war,

I believe we should take it. Thanks to the warning we have received, our military forces can be alerted and all preparations made to stand off assault or wage war, if necessary."

THERE followed a short, heated debate, with Secretary of War Wade championing the minority opinion that constitutional or unconstitutional, an attack should be launched upon Russia at once.

"Mr. Woodruff," said the President, "will you and your staff draw up this diplomatic protest immediately?"

"It should be signed by you, Mr. President," proposed the Secretary of State. "As Commander-in-Chief of the Army and Navy and Air Forces of the United States, addressed personally to Premier Solinski."

"I'll sign it," said the President. "And, as soon as it's dispatched, you'd better release this Mr. Gouchevisky. I'd like the Premier to hear from us, before he learns from his own representatives, that we know of Russia's intentions. Meanwhile, I charge you members of the War Emergency Council to take such steps and issue such orders as are necessary to put all forces on a war footing."

By the time Ellen reported for work in the morning, things were buzzing in the capitals of the world. Newspapers were out with smashing headlines, announcing that a diplomatic protest carrying a threat of war had been sent to Moscow after it had been ascertained by the United States that Russia had scheduled a surprise attack.

Military intelligence had decided that worldwide publicity would be the greatest temporary protection against Russia's contemplated act of aggression. As a consequence, full facts were given out with Andrew Brownell's name prominent in the news story. The rising young statesman was given credit for having unearthed, on his trip abroad, irrefutable evidence of Russia's military intentions—which evidence had been further substantiated through sources at home.

"Petrov Gouchevisky, attaché of the Russian Embassy, was detained for some hours last night by the F.B.I. and officials of the United States Military Intelligence," read the news account, "but released early this morning. His detention was part of a sweeping investigation made by the Government as a protective measure.

"Mr. Gouchevisky indignantly protested his arrest, terming it a breach of international law as applying to members of the diplomatic corps. He was supported in this contention by Ambassador Mitoff, who was not permitted to see his aide until he was freed this morning.

"There is rumor of an attractive American woman being involved in this situation but full particulars are being withheld at present.

"The entire international scene is filled with high explosive possibilities, as of this moment.

"Once again the question is raised—will we have peace or war?

"What transpires within the next twenty-four hours may decide."

REPORTERS, sensing a series of sensational news breaks, dogged the Russian Embassy and State Department offices. A number of them camped in the office of Andrew Brownell, central figure in the present war-scare flare-up.

"I'm sorry, gentlemen," declared Katherine Barker, Mr. Brownell's secretary, "you are wasting your time here. Any new developments will be announced by Secretary of State Wood-ruff. My boss has nothing to say."

"We'll stick around anyway," said the skeptical newsmen.

Dan Darrow, the country's leading columnist on international affairs, did not content himself with "sitting it out." He had spent years "cottoning" the secretaries of high government officials and Katherine Barker had been one of his best confidential sources of inside information.

Dan, finding that Katherine's boss was out, walked into Andrew Brownell's private office and beckoned her to follow him.

"Come on, Kate," he said. "Give with some real news. Everything's popping around here. It's Fourth of July. You know plenty. Has Russia replied to our State Department ultimatum yet?"

"If she has, I haven't heard of it," said Katherine.

"Okay. What interests me more—is the woman angle in connection with Mr. Gouchevisky. There ought to be a hot story there. It's being hushed up through regular channels. Do you know who the woman was?"

Katherine hesitated. "Dan—I can't talk."

"Listen, Baby—have I ever put you on the spot? No one will ever know where I got the information. Let's have it."

"Well—she's a White House secretary."

"That so? And she was running with the Russian?"

"Yes—they've been seen in public places together."

"How do you rate that? A pipeline from the White House—right into the Russian Embassy."

"It's worse than that," said Katherine. "This same woman's been going with Mr. Brownell."

"Kate—I could kiss you! This story is fantastic! It's wonderful!"

"Remember, Dan—I've got to have full protection on this one," warned Katherine. "I shouldn't be telling you—but I've never liked this woman. I have reasons to believe she's a double-dealer."

"You think she's been selling out her country?"

"I can't say as to that, but it's very strange to me—her playing up to Mr. Brownell and going with Mr. Gouchevisky, too. Not to mention her being a presidential secretary. Judge for yourself what a woman like that could do, if she had a mind."

"If she had *half* a mind," said Dan. "Don't spoil this story now, Kate—does the woman have sex appeal?"

KATHERINE nodded. "Lots of it. And she uses it. Oh, she's clever and talented, too. You'd have to be to interest a man like Mr. Brownell."

"Listen," complimented Dan. "He didn't do so badly when he picked his secretary."

Katherine's face colored but she liked it—and Dan knew it. "I suppose you want the woman's name?" she asked, lowering her voice.

"I've been patiently waiting, Baby," said Dan.

"It's Ellen Hopper."

"Hopper… Why, sure, I know her. I've chinned with her several times at the White House. Dark eyes, dark hair…nice figure…personality and stuff…"

"Dan—stop it," cried Katherine, impulsively.

"I catch," said the capitol's Number One columnist, shrewdly. "Something nice and personal between you two…none of my business, so we won't dig into that. But this was the girl who was picked up last night with Gouchevisky *at* his apartment?"

Katherine nodded. "The rest of the story's up to you. I haven't anything more to say."

"You've said plenty, Baby—and I won't forget you for this," said Dan. "I'll even this favor up, somehow."

Katherine smiled, nervously. "I'm not worrying about that—but you'd better be getting out of my boss' office—he's due back soon and I don't want him to know you were here."

"Okay." Dan opened the office door and sauntered out. Reporters from the Washington Star and Post were waiting in the anteroom. "Hello, boys," he greeted. "No news. I've just been giving Miss Barker the third degree—and she won't talk. Won't even give me an opinion about the weather."

"Don't hand us that, Danny boy," said Ed Porter of the Star.

"Come on, Miss Barker," called Sid Evans of the Post. "What incubates?"

"Nothing," said Andrew Brownell's secretary. "Nothing at all."

"No newspaper man ever believes another," laughed Dan, as he walked out. "I wonder why?"

CHAPTER SEVEN

A REPLY from the Russian government was not received until near the end of the twenty-four hour limit specified by the State Department.

It was a vitriolic denial of all charges and "implications" contained in the United States' note.

Russia had no thought or intent of attacking the United States but was greatly disturbed that such a fear should be expressed and such an attitude of belligerency should be revealed on the part of a nation hitherto considered as friendly."

Because of this "open accusation," Russia was recalling her Ambassador Mitoff and staff to Moscow until such time as cooler tempers and better relations might exist between the two countries.

However, refusal of the United States to accept Russia's disavowal of all charges made, would leave only one course of action open—*war.*

In an atmosphere of deep foreboding a second night session of the War Emergency Council was held.

"Attack at once! Don't take time to answer Russia's note!" demanded Secretary of War Wade. "It's absolute suicide, if we do!"

But calmer heads prevailed. Once again, the State Department's youngest diplomatic member saw his recommendations.

"I think we can gamble that no Russian attack will come— unless we force it—until her Embassy members have left the country. We are keeping a close watch on them. Their plane at the airport is being fueled. From such advices as we can get, they intend to take-off on Wednesday night. That's three days from today.

"I understand, from Miss Hopper, that this trip to Russia had been planned in line with the scheduled attack. In other words, Ambassador Mitoff and party would have flown back to Russia whether recalled or not. Their recall is thus apparently a 'blind.' Russia is adhering to her already established program and may attack us at the very moment expected. On the other hand, knowing we are now prepared to meet such an assault, Russia may postpone action—if assured that we, ourselves, will not 'jump the gun.'

"I therefore propose that we send a second note to Russia—in a conciliatory vein—expressing regret if information obtained by us, seemingly authoritative in nature, has proved erroneous. But explain that, because of the action being taken by Russia in withdrawing her Ambassador, we have no choice but to take like action. Express the hope that a speedy new understanding be arrived at, for the peace of mind of the citizens of both countries—and the peoples of the world. We can suggest that the Embassy staffs of any three foreign countries be appointed an Investigation Committee with power to determine whether or not either Russia or the United States is on the verge of attacking the other and to so report, if the facts warrant."

Secretary of Aviation Carlton opposed this last suggestion.

"All Russia has to do is appoint three of her satellite countries, friendly to her, to make an investigation and report to us. Do you think we could depend on that information?"

"No," said Andy. "But let Russia agree to have the Embassy staffs of three countries, known to be allied with us, to investigate her and we will agree to let three countries allied with Russia to investigate us."

"I object!" shouted Secretary of War Wade.

"Then you want war and *not* peace," charged the State Department's white-haired boy.

SECRETARY Woodruff got to his feet. "Just a moment, gentlemen. I may say here that, in the last twenty-four hours, we've been under tremendous pressure from various groups and big business interests. They naturally want their properties and holdings protected at home and abroad. There seems to be a widespread feeling that war with Russia is inevitable. Perhaps it is. God knows this period of uncertainty has dragged on for years. I think we should be prepared to protect American interests—but I'm more concerned with protecting American lives. What Mr. Brownell is proposing would indicate our sincerity. It would call Russia's bluff, *if* Russia is bluffing. If she won't agree to such a proposition—then it should be plain to us that she means to attack on schedule. Under those circumstances I would say—the sooner we attack, the better."

The support of his Chief brought a vote in favor of the procedure outlined by Andy.

"Draw up this second note and get it off at once," ordered the President.

The following morning, Washington and the world-at-large, had something else to think about.

Dan Darrow's "Cross-Roads of the World" column contained a scorching feature article, entitled:

FROM WHITE HOUSE TO STATE DEPARTMENT TO RUSSIAN EMBASSY!
A Double-Dealing, Double Play Combination
NO SECRETS "SAFE AT HOME"

The story went on in its blistering fashion:

One of Washington's top scandals of the century was revealed last night when facts came to light concerning the romance of an attractive White House Secretary with an equally handsome Attaché of the Russian Embassy.

The girl, Ellen Hopper, is understood to have been a favorite secretary of the President and to have enjoyed the confidence of many of the high officials in government.

She was particularly friendly with Andrew Brownell, Assistant to the Secretary of State, who just returned from an important foreign mission and brought back information that Russia intended attacking the U. S.

Miss Hopper, for the past year and more, has been seen in public, either in company with Petrov Gouchevisky of the Russian Embassy or Andrew Brownell of the State Department.

This, in itself, should have caused eyebrows to lift and questions to be raised. But Miss Hopper must have been an un- usually fascinating young woman to have captivated two brilliant men—one a Russian and the other an American. Even more so, to have communed with them openly, with no suggestion of secrecy.

Nothing is so disarming as public association with prominent figures. But Miss Hopper overstepped the bounds of propriety in her "romance of two worlds" when she was found in company with Petrov Gouchevisky in his apartment the other night, when the Russian attaché was picked up by the F.B.I. and Military Intelligence and taken in for questioning.

So far as can be learned, no action has been taken against Miss Hopper and none contemplated. She was at her desk in the White House, as usual, the following morning. But high officials saw to it that her name was left out of all news stories relating to this Gouchevisky episode—which leads to one pertinent question—*why?*

If certain State secrets have been leaking to Russia, in these most critical times, it is not possible that Miss Hopper has been the source of such leaks? Is the face of the State Department red? Is this why Miss Hopper is being shielded? Is Andrew Brownell embarrassed at this latest turn of events? There is more here than meets the eye—and ear.

Shouldn't this strange situation be investigated?

ELLEN was at work when Polly Wiggens, in charge of White House secretaries, placed the paper on her desk, pointing to the column.

"I don't believe you've seen this," she said. "The girls are all talking. It's early yet—but when the President comes in, you're sure to hear from him. But is this true, Ellen? Were you actually the girl who—?"

Ellen was reading the account with growing horror and dismay.

"This is terrible," she cried. "Terrible!" Her telephone commenced ringing. She placed the receiver to her ear. "No, no...it's not true...not the way it's written up... Hello... Oh!"

It was Katherine Barker on the wire.

"Ellen—Mr. Brownell wants you to come to the State Department right away. Very important."

"Yes," said Ellen, crushed. "I—I'll be over—in just a few minutes."

She hung up and finished reading the item as the other young women in the secretarial office looked on, some sympathetically, a few indignantly.

"She's been riding for a fall for a long time," one of them whispered. "Clear out of her class, playing around with those men. She'll catch it now."

Ellen looked up at the veteran, older woman, Polly Wiggens.

"I guess there's nothing for me to do but leave—before I'm fired," she said, gathering up her belongings.

"If you're not really guilty of anything, why quit?" said Polly. "This may all blow over. Everybody in public life gets attacked in the press at one time or another. It's all a question of whether you feel you can take it."

Ellen got up, pushed the chair under her desk, cleared off the top and packed in the drawers.

"All right, Polly," she said. "I'll leave my things here and we'll see what happens. I won't decide what to do until I get back from Mr. Brownell's office."

So saying, Ellen walked from the room, head held high, with every eye following her.

Ten minutes later, two women who openly despised one another, were meeting face to face. This time the secretary of Andrew Brownell had her rival just about where she wanted her.

"Just have a seat, Miss Hopper. Mr. Brownell is busy at the moment. Nice morning, isn't it?"

"What's nice about it?" said Ellen, pointing to a newspaper on Katherine's desk, opened to the Dan Darrow column.

"Oh," said Katherine, "you're referring to *that*. I was referring to the *weather.*"

"Not from the tone of your voice," rejoined Ellen. "Or your expression, either. I presume you found the article quite amusing?"

Brown eyes looked into green ones—and the green ones wavered.

"No," said Katherine, a bit upset by Ellen's directness. "Amusing isn't quite the word...but I did think you might have been a little more...shall we say discreet?"

"I can see that you feel extremely sorry for me," observed Ellen, ironically.

"On the contrary," said Katherine, "I feel sorry for Mr. Brownell. This news story has placed him in a most awkward position."

Ellen smoldered. "Are you implying that that's what he's called me to tell me?"

Katherine folded up the newspaper and put it on a corner of her desk.

"I can't speak for Mr. Brownell, of course," was her reply. "But I should think..."

"Well, don't," snapped Ellen. "You might overtax yourself—and you'd be wrong, anyway."

A buzzer sounded and Katherine picked up some papers, heading for the private office.

"I'll tell Mr. Brownell you are here," she said, frigidly.

A telephone rang. The call was picked up inside and Ellen heard Andy's voice in the receiver.

"Yes, General... I know. Yes...I agree with you...very serious. I've already done that...she's waiting to see me right now..."

"General Monihan," guessed Ellen. Andy lowered his voice so that she missed some of his conversation. But she heard the sign off: "...it's the only thing we can do. I'll phone you back later."

Katherine appeared in the doorway.

"Mr. Brownell will see you now," she announced.

DID Ellen imagine it, or was there a sadistic glint in those green eyes? As she passed her, in the doorway, she gave her an elbow.

"Ouch!" said Katherine.

"Just returning your little jab, with interest," she replied, in a low voice.

Andy looked up, just in time to see an exchange of stabbing glances.

"Close the door, please, Miss Barker," he called. Then to Ellen, as they were alone, "What's the matter—anything wrong between you two?"

"Nothing that a good murder couldn't cure," said Ellen. "She's undoubtedly very efficient...and loyal...and devoted...but I just don't like her type, that's all. She feels the same way toward me, so I suppose..."

"Why, she's always spoken most highly of you," said Andy, obviously mystified. "I'm sure you must be mistaken."

"Oh, well, skip it," said Ellen. "It's really unimportant."

Their eyes met for an instant in a sober, concerned glance.

"Sit down," Andy invited. He arose and placed a chair close to him, at the corner of his desk, so they could converse in low tones.

Ellen noted another copy of the paper containing Dan Darrow's column spread out before him.

"You've seen this, of course?" said Andy.

Ellen nodded, not trusting herself to any comment.

"I'm trying to trace it down," Andy went on. "We thought we had this incident covered so it would get no publicity. I'm certain you wanted no newspaper notoriety. The service you rendered was not of a kind that ever looks good in print. But this story can be frightfully damaging in its inferences. The public reaction is going to be bad. Opponents will seize on this as a sample of misconduct in office—rank carelessness in the matter of State secrets. You can expect me to be pilloried but I can't take time to defend myself now, world conditions being what they are. Nor can I defend you."

Ellen was seated, leaning forward, eyeing him, steadily.

"I hope you understand," said Andy, feelingly. His frank blue eyes searched hers. "For the time being, you will have to undergo public condemnation with me. We simply can't make known the part you have played in this highly dangerous Russian situation, or disclose the romantic interests involved. It would only make matters worse."

"I can see all that," said Ellen, sympathetically. "You don't have to explain."

"But, Ellen," said Andy. "You will suffer far more than I. I've already had word from the White House. You have been discharged. This is being done to help abate public clamor."

"I thought that would happen," said Ellen, steeling herself. "I've my few personal things all packed. What else?"

"General Monihan has just phoned," continued Andy. "You are being picked up by Military Intelligence and investigated. A probe of your relations with Petrov Gouchevisky will be made. This will all be a surface action to satisfy critics of the Administration and calamity howlers. After this crisis is past, you will be given a clean bill of health."

Ellen smiled. "Is that all?"

Andy looked his relief. "Isn't that enough?" he asked.

"Nothing is too much if it serves the best interests of our country in a time like this," said Ellen. "And if it helps make your assignment any easier."

Andy reached over and gripped her hand.

"The hardest part is yet to come," he said, "for me, at any rate. I won't be able to see you from now on. As far as the world is concerned, if there ever was anything between us, there isn't any more. You will temporarily be an outcast. Public officials you formerly knew in government will shun you. They'll have to. But I love you, Ellen...I want you to know that. I love you more now than ever before...and when this rotten business is over..."

"Perhaps I'll know my own mind by then," said Ellen, through sudden, unbidden tears. "Goodbye, Andy—don't bother your head about me. I'll get along."

ELLEN jumped to her feet and ran out of the office. Her unexpectedly quick departure caught Katherine unguarded. She collided with her as she flung open the door.

Turning back to Andy, who had witnessed the incident, she said: "You approve of this kind of eavesdropping, I presume, Mr. Brownell?"

"I most certainly do not," rebuked Andy.

"Then you might start tracing this story leak in your own office," Ellen fired over her shoulder.

She left behind her a greatly embarrassed and alarmed Katherine, as she walked out of Andrew Brownell's life.

CHAPTER EIGHT

THE Washington scandal could not overshadow the war scare for long. News of Ellen Hopper's dismissal as White House secretary and an investigation being made of her relations with Petrov Gouchevisky was shunted to an inside page as Russia's answer to the United States' second note took all the headlines.

Again the Russian government made a categorical denial of all "accusations and insinuations" and countered by charging that the United States was scheming, through this proposed

Investigation Committee to unearth secret facts concerning Russia's military strength.

"We will not consent to such investigation, because Russia frankly doubts its sincerity," read a portion of the Soviet Union's reply. "The three investigating countries, unfriendly to Russia, need only render an adverse report for aggressive reasons of their own, and Russia is laid open to the same surprise attack she is now being accused of preparing.

"We regard this proposal as an attempt to justify in the court of world opinion, a possible undeclared assault by the United States upon our country.

"Investigations, in and of themselves, mean nothing, if the word of a government means nothing. Either our two great countries continue to exist on a basis of mutual confidence and trust—all lying propaganda and false rumors to the contrary notwithstanding—or we take such steps as each feels compulsory in any given situation and at any moment."

This answer to the United States' note had been forwarded through the Swiss Embassy, which had also handled the message to Russia, since diplomatic relations had been broken off, with recall of Ambassador Mitoff.

Interpreted by a hurriedly summoned conference of State Department and government officials, the Russian reply spelled W-A-R in capital letters—the only question remaining—"How soon?"

Ellen, taken in by Military Intelligence, had spent two hours, closeted with General Monihan who asked her "routine questions for the records" and then assured her "off the record" that the government greatly appreciated her invaluable services and he regretted that this news story had proved so damaging to her.

"This will all be made up to you later," he said, "but we are powerless, at present, for political and strategic reasons, to do other than we are doing."

Ellen accepted the statement without comment and returned to the seclusion of her apartment where she kept track of rapidly moving events by radio.

Shortly before Wednesday noon, the day of the announced departure of the Russian Embassy staff for Moscow, Ellen received a surprise telephone call.

"Are you ready to leave with me?" said a familiar voice.

"Pete," exclaimed Ellen, amazed.

"There is a place on the plane for you," said the former Russian in her life. "Your phone is probably tapped but I am risking it to tell you that I still love you."

It was a daring thing for Petrov to do, international relations being as strained as they were, and Ellen gasped.

"I—I frankly didn't think, Peter, that I'd ever hear from you again," she said, wondering what was behind the call.

"How could I ever forget such a bewitching and exciting evening as we had together?" said Petrov. "How delightfully we fooled each other—and how clever you were in outwitting me. I like cleverness in women. It makes me love you all the more."

"Stop it, Pete. You're joking," cried Ellen. "I shouldn't be talking to you. Why are you calling?"

"To sympathize with you, my dear. Such a quaint country you live in—a woman like you renders a patriotic service and they reward her by taking her job away and disgracing her publicly. In Russia we would name a day of the week after you, declare a national holiday, have a big party. You can still come with me. How about it?"

Ellen felt her pulse hammering in her temples.

"You must be intoxicated to be talking this way. I won't listen to you any…"

"Seriously, Ellen—I couldn't leave your country without apologizing for trying to kill you. It seemed so necessary at the time. By some strange fate, we are both still alive. I hope the future is equally kind."

"Pete," said Ellen, emotionally. "You know there's only one thing that means anything now—to us or to the world—peace between Russia and the United States. You're returning to Moscow—if our friendship has meant anything, despite our difference in viewpoint and nationality—won't you use whatever influence you have to help your fellow citizens understand us? To believe that the rank and file of Americans don't want war—that they'd like to live in peace with every nationality, every country?"

THERE was a moment's vibrant silence on the wire. Then, Petrov's voice, speaking solemnly said: "My dear...the peace of the world, unhappily, is not decided by the rank and file of any country's citizens. Peace or war is in the hands of the powerful governing few. It has always been so. If a dictograph is taking down my remarks on a wire recorder let your government make what it will out of them. I will soon be thousands of miles away, but perhaps you will remember our talks...perhaps, if our planet is not blown up, we will live to see great human changes, which must come..."

"Not Communism," cried Ellen, impulsively. "I'd sooner not live than surrender my freedom of thought, of speech, of action, the right to live my own life in my own way, to worship as I choose..."

"I am sorry," cut in Petrov. "The time has come to say 'goodbye.' But I should like to remind you—there is only one freedom the peoples of Europe and most of the world are interested in today—that is freedom from want and starvation. They will sacrifice all other freedoms for it—yes, even their self-respect, their bodies, their souls. If we do not give them this freedom they will take our other freedoms away from us in time. I have never seen anything more frightening than a hungry mob. No form of government can stand too long against it. Don't ever forget—most humans think with their stomachs, and when their stomachs are empty—but, I'm saying too much. Goodbye, Ellen—and please do not think too unkindly of Petrov Gouchevisky."

The receiver clicked up before Ellen could make reply. She sat, for an instant, nerves still tingling from the unexpected shock of the call and the nature of the conversation. She had no doubt but that Military Intelligence had recorded every word and that what had been said would be carefully studied.

"They'll hardly expect these kind of thoughts passing between us," reflected Ellen. "I know it's probably unpatriotic to even think it—but I'll always consider Petrov one of the most interesting personalities and one of the finest minds I've ever met. Yet, with such a mind, how can he support the Russian system? There are so many things in this life I just can't understand."

Within an hour, Ellen received a second surprise phone call. This time it was from the State Department, Andrew Brownell, himself, calling. His voice, usually poised, had a quality of suppressed excitement in it.

"Ellen—tell me—what was that you said the other day about your grandmother—her prediction of a Great Light appearing in the sky?"

"Well, as I recall it," said Ellen, wonderingly, "it was just a story mother told, many times, to us children. But she always told it as though she believed it. She insisted that a Great Light would appear at a time when Man had made such a mess of things on earth that he couldn't see his way out."

"Go on. Anything else?"

"Well, yes—but this is even more incredible. Mother said that God-like beings would arrive on our planet at that time, to help us poor humans."

"Very remarkable," said Andy. "Where did your mother get this story? Did she make it up?"

"No, she claimed a Green Man came here, by space ship, when she was a young girl and that he told her this would happen. I guess few people believed such a thing then. Why are you suddenly so interested?"

"Because, Ellen," declared Andy, no longer masking his excitement, a "Great Light *has* appeared—it's spreading all over the Eastern Hemisphere right now—after sundown. Sidney, Australia, Tokyo, Shanghai, Calcutta and other places have reported it…and it's coming this way."

"No, Andy—I—I can't believe it…"

"It's true, Ellen. Russia is so concerned about it that she's officially requested us to hold off any possible contemplated attack, promising that she'll do likewise."

"Oh, Andy—that's wonderful!"

"Don't know whether it is or not—till we see what the Great Light's going to do to us," replied Andy. "All countries are mobilizing—this could be an attempted invasion of our planet from space. If it isn't, they say the Light is so terrific that the whole world is apt to be thrown into a state of panic."

"Not mother," cried Ellen. "Just wait till she finds out about this. I wish I were out on the coast with her right now."

"Ellen," cut in Andy. "The news on this phenomenon will soon be released on press and radio. It's been withheld up to now because it's seemed too fantastic—too frightening. Everything is being done to try to allay the wave of fear this Great Light is causing. The President is going on the air to declare a National Emergency and Martial Law. Nearly everyone will be out, looking up at the heavens at sundown. Will you go to the Lincoln Memorial with me, so we can see this together?"

"Of course! When?"

"I'll call for you before dark."

"Fine, Andy. But—wait a minute—is it safe for us to be seen together?"

Andy laughed. "Do you think anyone will notice us at a time like this?"

CHAPTER NINE

DESPITE every effort of press and radio authorities, working in co-operation with United States Government officials, it was impossible to avert hysteria as newspapers and airwaves announced the coming astronomical event.

Andy and Ellen, standing at the end of the Lagoon near the Lincoln Memorial could feel this wave of fearsome emotion.

"How long do you suppose this Light will stay with us?" asked Ellen. "Andy, I'm getting scared."

"*You*—scared?" said a voice at her elbow. "I will never believe that."

Ellen turned, to look into the smiling face of Petrov Gouchevisky.

"Peter," she exclaimed. "Why, I thought…"

"Flight cancelled," said the Russian. "How can any plane fly in a Light like that? It would blind everybody. No, I am very happy to stay on the ground—as long as the ground stays under me," Petrov glanced at Andy. "How do you do, Mr. Brownell? I hope this Light is not one of your new war weapons. If so, it is most effective."

Andy shook his head. "No, unfortunately, we can't claim it. We're no match for the cosmos."

"Which is no doubt a good thing," said Petrov. "For the first time tonight, I can relax knowing that we're not trying, at the moment, to outsmart each other."

Ellen had always liked Petrov's frankness. She sized them up—illumined as their features were—by the Light. Both strong, forceful, clean-cut men, with rapier minds, employed by their respective governments to fence with words until it again became necessary to resort to arms. Why should two such talented men have to live in two worlds of opposing ideologies? Why couldn't the peoples on this planet ever get together on a basis of common understanding? Why must one great power always be fighting another for supremacy? You could predict the end from the beginning. Defeat and degradation for the one—then, birth of a new power—the same battle over again—generation after generation—millions and millions killed—fine young men like Petrov and Andy—who might have done something constructively worthwhile for the world.

"Andy," cried Ellen, suddenly moved. "Why can't you and Petrov forget you are diplomats tonight—and just be *friends!*"

"If you'll come with me to my apartment I have some excellent vodka," suggested Petrov.

Andy hesitated. "No, thanks, Mr. Gouchevisky. I must remain within reach of my office. However, I'd like to really get acquainted some time—if our planet is still here."

Petrov smiled. "I know, Mr. Brownell, that Miss Hopper has a high opinion of you. Therefore, I must have, too. This Light—perhaps it will do no damage. At least, tonight, it permits us to part—as friends?"

Petrov extended his hand, which Andy, with a feeling of rivalry, took.

"If this Light fizzles out," he said, "we'll probably be shaking our fists at one another tomorrow. The Light hasn't changed anything—it's just postponed matters. Don't you agree, Mr. Gouchevisky?"

Petrov bowed. "Unhappily, Mr. Brownell, you are right." He turned to Ellen, taking her hand. "Good night, Miss Hopper. I am going back to my penthouse and drink a toast to the Light. May it keep our two countries from jumping at each other's throats."

He turned, with military bearing, and strode off, shielding his eyes against the Light.

Andy, watching him go, remarked, thoughtfully: "Every inch a diplomat, that fellow."

Ellen sighed. "I was in hopes you'd say that Petrov seemed like a fine person. If we don't start judging the individual and not the race pretty soon we're never going to get along with anybody."

HARRY HOPPER, II, had always considered his mother "just a little bit touched in the head." As he had grown to manhood, he had begun to doubt, more and more, her fantastic story of the visit of the Green Man to earth and his prophecy of the appearance, one day, of a Great Light.

The story was harmless enough so perhaps his mother should be humored. After all, she had led a nerve-racking life with his father, who should have been killed a hundred times before he finally vanished forever on his attempted rocket flight to the moon.

That Harry Hopper, II, had also gone in for aviation, had not helped his mother's nerves any. But now, at last, he had a safe job with Amalgamated Airlines, as General Manager of their Far Western Division. His days of taking chances were over, he was a settled married man. Now the only thing his mother had to worry about was what might happen to her two grandchildren.

But when Harry, II, came home from an evening out and learned from Harry, III, and daughter Annabelle that they'd been told the story of the Green Man and the Great Light, he was more than slightly provoked, especially when they hardly slept all night, for thinking and dreaming about it.

"Now, mother," he said the next morning. "You seem bound and determined to pass that yarn on to posterity. Folks may have believed that kind of stuff when you were a girl but today—well, it just makes you look foolish, that's all."

"Foolish or not," rejoined Grandma Hopper, with all her old-time spunk and vitality, "I'm going to keep on telling it. I may not live to see the Great Light, Harry—but I've a definite feeling that you and your children will."

Harry, II, looked at her. "I guess it's no use," he said. "You're worse than a religious fanatic. This is your story and you're going to stick to it. But please don't repeat it to the children, mother. I want to sleep nights."

Harry, II, did sleep—until the night of the Great Light. Then he stayed wide-awake and pop-eyed with the peoples of the entire world. And Grandma Betty Hopper, seated bundled up in the little garden behind the house, proclaimed long and loud to neighbors and all within hearing, as she pointed her cane at the sky: "I told you so! Not a soul would believe me—not even my own son—or my grandchildren—but there it is, glory be—the Great Light! It came, just as my Green Man friend said it would—to save us sorry humans on this earth. There's going to be a lot come of this—you mark my words. A terrible lot.

And the folks who haven't been doing right—who've been piling up all this misery and bringing on wars—they'd better look out! The Green Man'll be after them—he and his helpers. They won't show those kind of people any mercy. You mark my words. *Just mark my words!"*

Grandma Hopper's declarations and dire warnings chilled the marrow of every already chilled and trembling backbone. Her words struck home now, with devastating force and, for once, a prophet was not without honor in her home town—or the world, for that matter—because news of her prognostications reached press and radio, causing millions of soul-searching humans fearsomely to ponder what fate awaited them. And well they could think about such matters.

THE Great Light had now encompassed the globe, leaving fear and consternation in its wake. Two and a half billion human creatures had been shaken physically, mentally and spiritually. Here was something with which they could not cope—something beyond man's power to fight back. All they could do was hope and pray that this Great Light was not the forerunner of unspeakable catastrophe that each human, wherever he might be, would not be singled out and punished for some real or imagined wrong. Could it be possible that there was a personal God after, all—and that the day of His Second Coming was at hand? Thousands of different sects gathered in churches and cemeteries, awaiting the Resurrection. Last minute conversions were taking place in all faiths, everywhere. If the world was to be destroyed by fire—no one wanted to burn in Hell. All this as pitiful evidence of how little removed Man still was from ignorance and superstition.

It was midnight in Washington, D. C., one hour after the Great Light had reached the West Coast, when it happened.

Humans all over the North American continent heard the Voice. It came out of the atmosphere, seemingly close to them- —startlingly close—and yet it was clearly originating from far away. Every individual heard it, wherever he was, indoors or out, the Voice undiminished in volume. No radio broadcasting could approach such remarkable projection. Every activity ceased as the Voice spoke, in perfect English.

* * *

"Greetings—all peoples of Earth!

"Fear not—we come to help, not to harm you.

"The time for the Great Change on your planet has arrived.

"Things are never to be as they were again.

"You are to be freed from the age-old chains of Ignorance, Intolerance, Lust, Tyranny and Bigotry forever.

"We are a friendly host from the planet of Talamaya, who long since have won the individual freedom, which millions of you now seek but have failed to attain.

"We have come, at this time, to help you save the human race from annihilation and to establish a real Brotherhood of Man on this earth.

"One word of warning. Our Orders are to be LAW!

"Since you would destroy yourselves without our aid, any attempt to resist us will result in the destruction of your planet. We have only to alter the vibration of this Light, causing it to react upon the magnetic inner core of your earth, to bring about its instant disintegration.

"Watch the Heavens. You will shortly see us approaching your planet in our silver-colored space ships. We are coming in force as a demonstration of Power but only one space ship will land at each capital of each Nation, bearing a Leader with whom you are to co-operate.

"This Leader will speak your native language and possesses a knowledge of your country's history from its early beginning. He is well acquainted with all your problems as a nation.

"Your Rulers will then be advised of the Program you are to follow. Meanwhile, remain quietly in your homes or at your posts of duty—and await instructions.

"I will talk to you, from time to time, and you will hear from your own Rulers over your radio networks.

"Do as you are told and all will be well with you.

"Enjoy now a three day holiday while this New World Program is put into operation.

"I, Numar, your Liberator, have spoken!"

THE Voice had scarcely died away in the atmosphere when a great clamor arose over the surface of the earth. All tongues wagged in excited profusion. Rulers of all nations, large and small, called hurried conferences of every department of government.

"This is an INVASION FROM SPACE!" sounded a cry heard round the world.

But how to combat it? Although the Great Light had disappeared with sunrise in some of the far eastern countries, it had left all humans shattered in nerve and body. There was fear now of its returning at nightfall—fear, too, of the arrival of promised space ships—and even more dire happenings.

Astounded hearers of the Voice, on check-up, discovered that this Voice spoke in German over Germany, in French over France, in Italian over Italy, in Chinese over China, in Japanese over Japan, in the various Russian dialects over different sections of Russia, and so on. But, except in the case of the Voice, which spoke English—every other Voice, speaking simultaneously, signed off with the statement:

"I, speaking for Numar, your Liberator, have spoken!"

It was evident, then, that this Numar, whoever he was, served as "Commander-in-Chief" of this invasion. It was further presumed that he intended to land, in his spaceship, at Washington's Municipal Airport and proceed to the United States' capitol, to confer with that nation's top executives.

All very mysterious and shocking.

Andy and Ellen heard the Voice as they were walking up Pennsylvania Avenue toward the White House, in the crowds of highly excited humans, stretching from curb to curb. The Great

Light was at its height of brilliance as the Voice spoke, leaving not a shadow anywhere. People stood, shoulder to shoulder, examining each other's faces, seeking courage in mob companionship. As the Voice finished speaking and the terrific tension was broken, some sobbed, others laughed hysterically, still others had fainted and a few, screaming frenziedly, tried to escape the penetrating rays of this Great Light.

"Come on," said Andy, pushing Ellen toward a side street. "This is no place for us. People are going mad before this night is over. Lots of them have already. Let's get back to your apartment."

Ellen was trembling, lips quivering, almost ready to break herself.

"Oh, Andy, this is simply terrific...no words to describe it... I'm frightened as I've never been before."

"We haven't been harmed yet," said Andy, grimly. "That's what we have to remember when things we've never experienced before are happening. This Power has declared itself to be friendly. We'll have to accept that statement as true because we can't do anything about it. I'll have to leave you at home and get to my office. Every local, state and national executive will be getting together for a conference after this."

Ellen stopped suddenly and clutched his arm.

"Andy," she cried. "Mother's prophecy again! The God-like beings she said would arrive on our planet—to help us! Remember?"

"Ellen," said Andy, "it's evident to me that your mother knows more about what's happening now than any other human on this planet. She can be extremely helpful. You're not going home—you're going with me to the White House—and we're phoning your mother and letting her talk to the *President!*"

AS ANDY had anticipated, official cars were parked three deep around the White House, which seemed spotlighted in the radiance of the heavenly illumination. Photographers were shooting pictures in what should have been "the dead of night" without the aid of any flash bulbs. News reporters were covering their "beats" as normal, despite the fact that many felt this might be "their last assignment." Important personages were arriving constantly and scurrying into the White House after being checked at the door by secret service men and a special heavy guard of soldiers, at each entrance. The whole scene had the air of war times. Anxious thousands had been roped off—humans who had pathetically converged upon the White House to futilely appeal to their government to "do something about this Great Light."

When Andy and Ellen were ushered into the Conference Room, they found it jammed. President Norman Ellsworth was in his chair at the head of the long table, looking greatly troubled and not a little terror-stricken.

"Gentleman," he was saying, "we are meeting tonight to discuss ways and means of facing a threat far more serious than a possible surprise attack by Russia. Everyone, I am certain, heard this strange message. The peoples of all other countries heard it at the same time. It is the consensus of opinion of those whom I have already consulted that this is an ingenious invasion by Beings who intend to trick us into surrendering peacefully, under the guise of helping us. You perhaps noted that one of these Beings is being dispatched, as a Leader, to confer with the rulers of each Nation—and the Being in charge of all is apparently coming here. I am open to suggestions as to how we may plan to cope with this unparalleled situation."

The President produced a handkerchief and dabbed at a dripping brow. He glanced about him at faces as covered with nervous perspiration as his own.

"Mr. President," addressed Andy, standing up in the rear of the room.

"Mr. Brownell," recognized the Chief Executive, as all looked wonderingly in the direction of the State Department's ace troubleshooter.

"I believe I have come upon a source, which can help us understand what is happening," announced Andy.

There was an instant scraping of chairs as gold braid, brass hats and top civilian executives prepared to give fixed attention.

"I've brought with me," continued Andy, pointing to Ellen who stood beside him, "Miss Ellen Hopper, *former* White House secretary. Many of you know her." There was a murmur of comment. "I think I can say now that she was grossly misjudged several days ago—but there's no time to comment about that now. It so happens that Miss Hopper's mother, who resides in La Canada, California has predicted, for years, just what is taking place at the present time."

Conferees glanced unbelievingly at one another, several laughed, nervously; a few openly guffawed their disbelief.

"A fortuneteller, eh?" said someone.

"No," replied Andy, with great seriousness. "Mrs. Hopper claims to have seen and talked with a Green Man who came to this earth in a spaceship when she was a young woman—who told her this Great Light would appear—and that Beings from space would arrive to help straighten out affairs here."

Secretary of War Wade jumped to his feet.

"Great God, gentlemen," he cried. "Are we going to waste precious time with a spatial enemy about to land all over this planet, listening to such nonsensical drivel as this?"

"It's not drivel," Ellen found herself speaking out. "My mother's a sane and sensible woman. She's told me this story since I was a little girl. I didn't know whether to believe her or not—but I never forgot it—and I believe her now."

"Mr. President," addressed Andy. "If what we are telling you is true wouldn't it be wise—before deciding on a course of action—to get Mrs. Hopper on the long distance phone and for you to talk with her—and learn all you can about her experience as it has a bearing on this emergency?"

"Yes, yes!" supported a chorus of voices. "Do that! Let's hear what she has to say! Go ahead!"

"Please have Miss Hopper come forward," requested the President, "and put in a call for her mother. I'll be glad to speak with her."

ANDY escorted Ellen to the head of the table where a place was made for her beside the President as she took up the phone and placed the call.

"She's ringing them," Ellen reported, after a minute, "but there's no answer. They're probably out in the yard, looking at the Light, like everyone else…Ah! Here's someone…it's my brother… Hello, Harry? This is Ellen… Yes, isn't it terrific? What's that? Mother's not crazy after all…? I'll say she's not… Listen, Harry, I'm talking from the White House… I'm calling for the President…he wants to speak to mother… Will you get her to the phone…? Sure, I'll hang on. How's little Harry and Annabelle…? Scared to death…? No…? Okay, Harry…"

Ellen turned to the now tremendously interested top executives.

"Harry says his kids think it's wonderful—better than Fourth of July fireworks! He says their Grandmother told them not to worry—that everything's going to be all right—and they believe her."

"Wish *we* did," said someone, and there was a burst of nervous laughter.

"Hello…is that you, Mother?" said Ellen into the phone. There was a long wait at Ellen's end of the line as she listened, while an excited woman's voice could be heard going on and on. "Yes, of course, mother, I remember…of course… I'll never doubt you again… Never… You bet I'm tickled that you lived to see it… Listen, mother…wait a minute… Mother, the President wants to speak to you… Yes…he wants you to tell him what you know about the Green Man and the Great Light…tell him what you've told me and your grandchildren and everybody…here, Mother, the next voice you hear will be the President of the United States."

Ellen, laughing, passed over the phone to the Chief Executive.

"Mrs. Hopper," he started, but this was as far as he got. He sat, with his eyes growing wider and wider, listening. Suspense built up in the conference room as President Ellsworth, nodding and wiping his forehead, tried again and again to slip in a word or a question.

"You don't say," he finally began exclaiming, as his jaws dropped open and his eyes now bulged. "You don't say… You DON'T say… Well… That's amazing, Mrs. Hopper, it really is," he managed, as she either ran down or ran out of breath. "Thank you very much. You've rendered a great service to your government…very great… What's that…? Yes, I'll remember you to the Green Man…and I hope *he* remembers *you.*"

The President put the receiver down and stared dumbfoundedly into space.

"Let's have it, Mr. President! What did she say?" cried several.

The Chief Executive stood up. "Gentlemen, this is incredible. Mrs. Hopper claims that her uncle, a great astronomer of some years ago, was visited by a Green Man from this very same planet, Talamaya that was mentioned in the message tonight. And what is more astounding, the Green Man's name was Numar—the exact same name as was given in this cosmic broadcast. It is quite evident, therefore, that this Mr. Numar, whom we'll now have to accept as having been on this earth before, is returning with an army of his fellow Green Men to take over control of this world. But Mrs. Hopper insists that Mister Numar's intentions are benevolent—that, just as he says, he means no harm. She further states that he is a most charming personage—that she enjoyed knowing him and that, if we mention her name to him, she feels it may have some influence." A great exchange of comment followed the President's condensation of his talk with Ellen's mother.

"Are you suggesting then, Mr. President?" questioned Secretary of State Woodruff, "that we assume a friendly, rather than a hostile attitude toward the Green Man—or perhaps I should say, Mr. Numar, when he arrives?"

"In the light of this information, I *would,*" declared the Chief Executive. "I recommend we constitute ourselves a welcoming committee and adjourn to the Airport to await Mister Numar's landing. The fact that he, himself, is coming to Washington means that he considers it the world's most important capitol. If we can't fight him, perhaps we can get on his good side through collaboration. I know of no other possible course. It's worth trying."

THE Secretaries of War, Navy and Aviation were not too pleased with this decision but could offer no plan of defense, since the Great Light was so bright as to prevent any aerial opposition to the invading airships.

"We may be going to our deaths, who knows?" said Secretary of War Wade. "I'd personally rather die, fighting back, as best we can."

"Henry," said Secretary of the Navy Hamlin, "I'm in hearty agreement with your sentiments—but we are totally unprepared to meet any attack from outside our planet. That's something nobody ever figured on."

"And just as we were getting ready to hit Russia, too," said Secretary of Aviation Carlton. "Personally, I'd prefer to battle against the Known, any day, than the Unknown. This has us licked before we start."

It was a chastened group of top governmental officials who entered limousines and, under military and motorcycle escort, were driven to the Municipal Airport, Andy and Ellen with them.

"Feeling any better?" Andy whispered.

"Yes, I am," said Ellen, "that talk with mother helped. She's so positive, Andy, that Mister Numar is coming here for a good purpose, I'm even beginning to look forward to meeting him."

"Well, it shouldn't be long now," said Andy. *"Listen..."*

They were nearing the Airport and, overhead, could suddenly be heard a high, musical sounding hum—not loud but pleasing to the ear, steady and rhythmic.

"Oh, Andy—*Look!*"

Passing low, only five hundred feet above them, flying in formation, were row on row of huge silvery aerial monsters, each easily a quarter of a mile long. They were cigar-shaped—pointed, glistening noses, flashing in the Great Light.

Secretary of Aviation Carlton, in the same car, took one look.

"We can scrap everything we've got in aircraft and rockets," he said. "They're not even toys compared to that."

As for President Ellsworth, his comment on alighting at the Airport was: "Yes, I can see very clearly that our best policy in dealing with Mister Numar is one of wholehearted co-operation."

CHAPTER TEN

WITHIN a short time, from every part of the United States and all foreign countries came excited reports of great aerial armadas having been sighted. Terrorized citizens demanded of their governments what they were going to do about it. The sky had seemed filled with these tremendous space ships, traveling at terrific speed.

Over the capitols of the various nations, these Goliaths of outer space were described as moving slowly, easily through the air like lazy, mammoth silver whales.

All humans, however, whether in the jungles of Africa or the icy wastes of the Arctic had opportunity to witness this horrific display of the space invaders' might. It was enough to convince all but the frenzied foolhardy that no power on earth could hope to survive against such superior strength.

The world's two greatest military powers, Russia and the United States, conversing now by long distance telephone, in friendly, co-operative mood agreed that each should submit, for the time being, to the landing forces of the Talamayans.

And so, the Premier of Russia and the President of the United States, each humbly but uneasily awaited the arrival of the visitors from space with whom they had been forcibly "invited" to collaborate.

"We may be surrendering our planet, for all time, to the whims of a crafty foe who will enslave us forever," said a high official gloomily. "But what else can we do?"

"There will be signs in the heavens and the sun will be darkened and the moon will not give forth its light," sang the religious fanatics. "God is sending His messengers to judge the world and all sinners in it. Prepare to meet your doom!"

Eye had not seen and ear had not heard the spectacle, which now occurred at the Airports of every nation's capitol, as in perfect synchronization of timing, one great space ship detached itself from its immediate protecting fleet and commenced to hover over a landing area below. Then, descending vertically like immense elevators, they settled upon the ground, these quarter mile length leviathans of the air making a musical purring sound.

President Ellsworth and his executive heads watched the silver monster come to rest as, in the sky above, other great mechanical birds circled.

A Voice suddenly spoke from out the atmosphere—as other Voices were speaking, simultaneously, in different languages, at foreign Airports.

"Warning—do not approach within fifty feet of this ship or you will be instantly electrocuted."

Awe-stunned spectators respectfully kept their distance— studying the amazing cone-shaped interstellar traveler. It looked not unlike a pointed-nosed fish of prodigious dimensions, which had just swum out of the sky. At rest, gill-like apertures rose and fell as though the gigantic whale were alive and breathing. A long paneled slit in each side revealed a section of the interior and obviously permitted visibility. But the vast inner chambers of this aerial vessel, with its actual motive power, were hidden and a complete mystery.

A GANGWAY suddenly shot out from a porthole, forward, and made contact with the ground. Then a silver door slid noiselessly back and, framed in its entrance stood a majestic figure, robed in white, luminous garments; similar tight-fitting headdress, and possessing bright green skin!

"The Green Man!" cried the welcoming committee, almost in one breath. "Mrs. Hopper was right!"

Descending the ramp, this figure advanced toward them, smiling, and extending his hand.

"My name is Numar," he introduced, "of the Planet Talamaya. Greetings!"

President Ellsworth, first in line, took the offered hand, not without considerable misgivings.

"My mime is Norman Ellsworth," he said, a bit tremulously. "President of the United States. I greet you on behalf of our government and its people."

"Thank you," smiled Numar, and looked beyond the Chief Executive, to the others assembled.

"And these," continued the President, "are mostly the heads of our different government departments."

"I should like to meet them," said Numar, "although I am already familiar with their records in office."

This announcement caused many in the welcoming committee to wince. But they were presented to the Visitor from Space by the President, one by one, each shaking his hand and being deeply impressed by the experience.

Last to meet Numar were Andrew Brownell of the State Department and the attractive young woman in his company.

"I've heard of you before," Andy informed, as he held Numar's hand.

"Yes," spoke up President Ellsworth, helpfully. "We've all heard of you—in fact, Miss Hopper here is the daughter of a woman who claims—that is—who actually—well, so she says— knew you the first time you visited this earth."

Numar turned to critically survey Ellen, with his dark, penetrating eyes.

"You do not look like your mother," he said.

"No," smiled Ellen, the tension breaking. "I take after my father."

THE GREEN MAN RETURNS

Numar returned her smile. "He was a most unusual man. It is regrettable that he was lost, trying to reach the moon."

"You—you knew that?" gasped Ellen.

Numar nodded. "I have always been interested in those who remembered me here," he said. "Your mother, especially. We had quite an experience together."

"So she's told me—many, many times," laughed Ellen, feeling more and more at home in the Green Man's presence.

High government officials, mouths agape, had been listening to this personal conversation. Numar's friendly attitude toward Ellen was most reassuring.

"We're mighty glad to have you visit this earth again," said President Ellsworth, putting on his most hospitable manner. "How—er—long do you and your—er—associates intend to remain?"

"Until our mission is completed," was Numar's prompt answer. "It all really depends upon how well the people and rulers of your earth co-operate. We are bringing a new Plan of Living to this world and it may not be too cordially accepted at first."

"I—I see," said the President, doubtfully. "Well, will you and your crew—and other members of your party come with us? We'll secure hotel accommodations for you. But I understand, from Miss Hopper's mother, that you don't eat?"

NUMAR smiled. "No—we are not human creatures like yourselves. We exist on air and water. As for hotel accommodations, our airship is equipped for us to live in. My associates will not leave the ship while we are here. I will go and come from it. Have no concern about us. We will take care of ourselves."

This left President Ellsworth groping for something to say—or to offer.

"It's rather late now—perhaps you'd like to retire after your long trip?" he finally proposed.

But he was taken aback anew when Numar replied: "We never sleep. The journey was not fatiguing. However, I presume you humans are tired?"

"We've had a somewhat trying day," the President admitted. "What with prospects of another world war—and then this Light. It has badly frightened most of our people. Isn't there some way it can be turned off?"

Numar shook his head. "It is being beamed at your Earth from our planet," he advised. "When every human has seen the Light it will disappear."

There was an awkward moment, during which Ellen felt that another personal comment might help.

"Mother wanted us to be sure and give you her regards," she said.

Numar rewarded Ellen with a smile.

"You will please convey my regards to your mother. Tell her that I hope to see her while I am on earth." Then turning abruptly to his awed welcoming committee, the smile faded as he said: "Shall we go now to the White House? The peoples of the world will not rest, Light or no Light, until they have heard from their rulers that all is well. It will do you no harm to spend a sleepless night. You may have many of them before the justice and peace and freedom, which was the original destiny of your human race is brought to pass."

In every world capitol a like scene was taking place. Representatives of Numar, the self-announced Liberator, Green Men like himself, were holding conclave with local Rulers and their assembled top executives. Each Leader from the Planet of Talamaya astounded his hearers by speaking their native tongue fluently and revealing a thorough knowledge of governmental affairs as they pertained to that nation, at home and abroad. It was realized, at once, that no subterfuge could be accomplished.

Numar's ride through the streets of Washington en route to the White House from the Municipal Airport, seated beside President Ellsworth, was the occasion for tremendous excitement as throngs of wild-eyed Washingtonians sought to catch a glimpse of him. Many fearsomely applauded; a few of the more defiant and courageous, booed.

PRESIDENT Ellsworth had invited Ellen Hopper and Andrew Brownell to ride with him, feeling more secure to have some connecting links with Numar's past visit present, for whatever helpful influence they might have.

"Has Washington changed much since you were here before?" Ellen asked, pleasantly, as they came within sight of the White House.

"The same old historic places," smiled Numar. "But mostly *new* people."

Andy nodded. "That's right, Mister Numar. I wasn't even thought of when you were previously on this planet."

Numar eyed the State Department's white-haired boy.

"You were in the Mind of the Great Creator, coming toward this planet in Time, as a part of the Great Unfoldment," he said, amused at Andy's expression of bewilderment. "You have an important role to play in your country's present destiny—as will soon be revealed to you. So has the daughter of my earth friend, Mrs. Hopper—whose name when I knew her was—*Betty Annabelle Bracken.*"

"Mister Numar," cried Ellen. "You are positively amazing. How could you remember that?"

Numar smiled. "My memory goes back some millions of years of your earth time. Some day your memories will extend that far—but you human creatures will then be in higher and more refined bodies and in another plane of existence. Death, you know, is no end of life—it is merely a means of transition from one evolving phase of life to another."

"We *don't* know that," said Ellen, glancing excitedly at Andy. "That's tremendously interesting, Mister Numar. I've always wanted to believe that this life was only the beginning...so many humans don't have a chance to develop here..."

"That is true," said Numar, sympathetically. "And it is because you human creatures have such a glorious destiny that we have come here to help you realize it. This planet was intended to prepare you for the Life Beyond. Instead, you humans have misdirected your forces, lost your way and were about to destroy yourselves. It is our task, in our present state of development, to go to the aid of creatures on such planets as yours when they lose the power to help themselves. The time has come for them all to see the Light!"

CHAPTER ELEVEN

UNIQUE in the history of life on this planet were the conferences now entered upon by the Green Men from Space with the Rulers and their Executive staffs of the nations of earth. And, because Numar, "Commander-in-Chief" of these Leaders, had elected to confer with the President of the United States and his departmental heads, world interest centered mostly upon the announced outcome of this all night session.

Once all high officials had been reassembled in the conference room and the doors locked to reporters and camera men, President Ellsworth called the meeting to order.

"Mister Numar has requested this opportunity to address us," he declared. "I have no advance idea of what he is going to say although he has assured me that he and his fellow Talamayans have come here, motivated only by a friendly interest in helping us—or, rather—the whole human race, save itself. I hope Mister Numar will forgive a little skepticism on that point because I know the Russians have been trying to put over a world system for saving humanity—and we've been just as set in trying to put over *our* system—and the Nazis of Germany tried to put over *their* system in the two previous world wars—and there's been nothing come of such efforts but more conflict, more hatred and prejudice and disunity between nations and peoples. If there's a workable plan for straightening out the mess we're in on this earth I'd be glad to hear it and I'm sure everyone in this room—and in the country would, too. You, Mr. Numar, must think you've got something or you wouldn't have come this far and put on all this display in the heavens—and brought along this force to back you up. On the other hand, you can't expect us to accept everything right off, if we don't approve."

Having ventured to go on record to this extent, President Ellsworth presented Numar to his country's top executives who stood up and paid tribute with their applause.

Ellen, assigned to transcribe all that would be said in this extraordinary session, sat at the head of the table with Andy. She sat, pencil poised, notebook open, looking up into the Green Man's unusually expressive face. If he had existed for some millions of years, earth time, his features and hands didn't show it. They fairly vibrated with vitality. His apparel seemed almost a part of his figure, so closely did it fit about him. He was perfect in stature, over six feet in height, erect and with a bearing of simple grandeur and poise, which commanded instant respect—even awe. This Being possessed great, unfathomed power, yet he deported himself with quiet dignity.

He was waiting now for the last chair to be scraped and the last nervous throat to be cleared, before he began. Illumination from the Great Light flooded through the windows, causing his green countenance to glow with a peculiar radiance.

"I have listened to the remarks of your President," he said, finally, "and I wish to say at the outset that this Plan of Living, which we are bringing to your Earth is workable because it has been successfully introduced on other planets where human creatures, not unlike yourselves, have failed to live up to the finer possibilities within them.

"Let me say further that you and all other world rulers have no choice in the matter. You must accept this Plan, as I lay it before you, and lend every co-operation toward putting it into immediate force and effect so that it can be carried out by all peoples. This is mandatory. Failure to co-operate will result in destruction of your planet, as I have previously warned, since you human creatures are headed toward self-destruction anyway but for our intervention."

THE silence in the conference room took on the atmosphere of a morgue. But out of this silence one voice dared to speak.

"Mister Numar," challenged the State Department's youngest diplomat. "Aren't you proposing, in forcing this Plan upon us, to trespass upon our Free Will, which we have been taught to believe is sacred? God has given the human creature Free Will and Free Choice—the power to decide for himself what is right and wrong, what he shall or shall not do. True, Man has made a great many mistakes—but it's been Man's fault, not God's. I'm wondering if Man still shouldn't be permitted to work out his own destiny—and to punish himself by self-destruction if he cannot find the answer to his problems? That, rather than be compelled to follow any Plan, which you or any other Strange Power might attempt to impose?"

A breathless assemblage awaited Numar's answer. The Green Man had listened attentively to Andy's well-stated protest and had not "struck him dead" for speaking out. Ellen, taking down Andy's words, flashed him a look of admiration.

"Exercise of Free Will, when a human creature has neglected development of his spiritual nature, leads to Free License," replied Numar, speaking slowly and choosing his phrases carefully. "Your Will is not free when it is owned, body and soul by Appetite—unbridled desire. Can any man think clearly who is intoxicated? Wrong desires bring about wrong expression of Free Will. Wrong thinking always produces wrong results. This Plan of Living will not trespass upon Free Will—it will liberate it so that Reason and Free Will can operate together. A drunken man has forfeited reason and cannot accomplish a good end for himself or others. The world is drunk with thoughts of power for power's sake. How many persons do you think actually possess Free Will today? Can you speak out against a church or a government or a prominent individual today whom you may believe to be corrupt? You, a diplomat, should best be able to answer that question? At your first public utterance, would you not be removed from office by your superiors who may agree with you, in private, but who dare not speak their minds in public?"

NUMAR paused. The face of the State Department's youngest diplomat was red. He had nothing to say.

"Then you do not now have real Free Will—you only think you have. It is hemmed in by all manner of influences and controls and private interests and you are a man walking a tightrope between the expedient and the inexpedient—what you know you dare not say and what you don't know you don't."

Numar smiled and placed a hand on Ellen's shoulder.

"I need go no further than this most recent example. This fine young woman was used by your Military Intelligence to secure some needed information from a man in the Russian Embassy. I happen to know—through channels of higher intelligence of which you humans are unaware—that Miss Hopper performed her mission satisfactorily.

"But, because an insinuating story was printed in the papers, suggesting embarrassing personal relations between Miss Hopper, the Russian gentleman and Mr. Brownell—did anyone here feel FREE to speak out in her defense? No—instead she was permitted to suffer public disgrace and was removed from office—all in the name of service to her country. This is but one little example of the depth of involvement of human relations, moral principles and so-called Free Will with the sordid influences in control of your planet at the present time."

The assemblage sat stunned, unable to answer Numar's charge, utterly dumbfounded at the extent of his personal knowledge. Each individual began, uncomfortably, to examine this own conscience, suddenly afraid of what he might find there and what this Green Man from the distant planet of Talamaya might reveal.

"The cure of these conditions," went on Numar, "is no longer possible through an attempt to apply *surface treatments*, which will not offend 'special interests', 'powerful international groups' or countries possessing opposing ideologies. Billions of dollars continually poured into Europe won't halt the spread of Communism or any other ism threatening the American way of life. While weak, dishonest governments prevail as well as poverty and lack of education among the masses all the world's money cannot change conditions.

"Only a New Plan of Living can save humanity—a new plan, which strikes deep, like a surgeon's knife cutting out cancer—removing some of the good flesh along with the bad so that the seeds of new and recurring cancer can be eliminated, at the same time, with the malignant growth.

"Do you think any government on this planet today has the power or the courage to take the drastic steps necessary to save not only itself, but all peoples of the world? No—the power-mad rulers, the selfish interests behind these rulers, and ignorant, misguided, hate-directed masses will destroy each other first, trying to preserve systems and practices, which can never bring them happiness, security or peace."

Numar paused as Ellen bent frantically to her shorthand notes in an attempt to keep pace. The Great Light, streaming in at the windows, was strong upon Numar's listeners, who squirmed uneasily in their seats.

"That is why," continued the being who had announced himself as the World's Liberator, "we have come to your Earth—to do for you what you can no longer do for yourselves.

"You, in the United States of America have reached the highest mechanical development in all history. You have achieved, through your production genius, the highest standard of living. You have become the wealthiest of all nations. Your remarkable Constitution has permitted you to be more free than any other humans. But in the face of all this you still have millions of underprivileged among you, the highest divorce rate in the world, a high percentage of crime, maladjustment and juvenile delinquency—indicating that you have been able to manufacture everything but happiness. Then something must also be wrong with your system of life and living—even as there are even greater ills existing in governments and nations abroad.

"I have a great and unique advantage over you human creatures. I can see you with a completely outside perspective and judge you as you cannot judge yourselves.

"You humans have gone as far as it is possible to progress on mind and energy alone. Drunk with your own sense of material power, you have developed the illusion that you are the creators of this Universe. When you split the atom, invented the atomic bomb and liberated atomic energy—you forgot that God, the one and only *real* Creator, was still behind all this—still Ruler of His sublime and unending and unimaginable Universe of universes. You decided that so-called spiritual power was a myth and that churches should only be used as organizations of influence to drug the minds and hearts of unthinking, trusting, ignorant humans. So the churches have joined the war against opposing ideologies in the name of God—and religion and politics and economics of people and countries have been mixed together in a bewildering stew, each party in power attempting to find the right recipe to appease the popular appetite at the moment.

"WHAT has been the result? Growing confusion, disorder, fear, hate and approaching chaos.

"And what remedy have the most brilliant minds of scientists, industrialists, politicians, economists, ministers and all other world leaders been able to conceive for such unspeakable conditions? *Another world war!*

"This is no remedy, gentlemen. Had you been permitted to attempt it—your planet and all human creatures on it, would have been no more."

Numar stopped speaking and quietly surveyed each face, in turn, of those who confronted him. They were tensely sober, sitting as though frozen to their chairs.

"I am now ready to present the new Plan of Living, which you are to adopt," Numar announced. "But, first, I should like to ask if there are any questions or comments?"

Again, the silence was profound. Numar, smiling, glanced at the youngest member of the State Department's staff.

"Mr. Brownell?" he inquired.

Andy stood up. It was obvious that he was deeply moved.

"I should just like to say," he declared, "that I have heard, for the first time on this earth, the truth, frankly and openly spoken, as none of us here or anywhere would have dared speak it. I agree with you that any real cure of this world's ills must strike deeper than any country, with its age-old traditions and customs and conflicting interests, prejudices and foreign entanglements, can possibly strike. I am willing to accept, on faith, after hearing your statement, that your interest in helping us right conditions on this earth is sincere. Therefore, I await your presentation of the new Plan of Living and pledge, in advance, my support—for I frankly confess that we have no solution for the existing world dilemma."

Andy sat down and put his face in his hands as a man who is relieved at having given voice, at last, to his true feelings. There was a stir in the conference room as if, for the moment, other government officials might give utterance to similar feelings—but none quite had the courage to so commit themselves.

"The Plan is this," spoke Numar.

"There is to be formed, at once, a United States of the World. A Constitution will be adopted, with its preamble patterned after your inspired Constitution of the United States. It will read, as follows:

"'We, the peoples of this planet, in order to form a more perfect union of all governments, establish justice, insure domestic and international tranquility, provide for the defense of all, promote the general welfare, and secure the blessings of liberty to ourselves and our posterity, do ordain and establish this Constitution for the United States of the World, based upon the following provisions...'"

THE impact upon the consciousness of those assembled was clearly evident.

"Magnificent," approved President Ellsworth. "A Constitution modeled after ours will be most acceptable."

"But some of the provisions may not be, at first," warned Numar, smiling. "I will not attempt, at this time, to quote them exactly. I will simply cover some of the main features of the Constitution.

"And, let me remind you that as I am speaking to you here, my representatives, as you would call them, are presenting this same Constitutional Plan to the rulers of all other countries. We shall expect ratification of this Constitution by tomorrow night so that preparations can immediately go forward toward full operation under it. This means setting aside all existing laws or regulations, which would ordinarily prohibit such action. I think all governmental heads will recognize the advisability of prompt co-operation."

There was a nodding of heads in acquiescence.

"The Constitution will outlaw all war for all time."

Numar's statement drew a burst of applause.

"It will establish the equality of all races," he continued, "with equal opportunity for education."

There was applause but with lessened enthusiasm.

"Because English is more widely spoken than any other language on earth, it is to be the universal language. Every human will be required to learn to read, write and speak it in addition to his native tongue in order that there may be communication, on a basis of common understanding between all races on this planet."

Numar smiled as he saw that this provision met with unanimous approval.

"To relieve, at once, the widespread poverty and degradation existing in many parts of the world today," he went on, "a subsistence will be guaranteed to all citizens at the subsistence level of each nation so that each human may possess the absolute necessities of life and be assured of basic security."

A stunned and wondering silence met this statement.

"Won't the cost of such a gigantic project bankrupt the world?" a voice finally called out, impulsively. Numar glanced in the direction of his interrogator and addressed Secretary of Agriculture Frank Faulkner.

"The billions already spent on past wars and armaments by all nations—and being spent now in preparation for a new war—together with the diversion of natural resources and food products into constructive channels, would feed, clothe and shelter every human creature as God intended that they should be provided for on this earth," was Numar's answer.

There was no further comment, and he proceeded:

"All life is to be divided into three periods. The first fifteen years, each human will be required to attain a high school education or its recognized equivalent."

Not a voice was raised, only amazed, questioning glances.

"The next twenty-five years—up to the age of forty, humans are to work at a trade or at physical labor or at preparation for entrance and service in professions such as medicine, engineering, government work, the care of home and children... Then," added Numar, "the second twenty-five years—after forty and up to sixty-five, the average life expectancy on this planet—there is to be *compulsory retirement* of all trade and physical workers for study, recreation, travel, intellectual and spiritual development, teaching, consultation service, entrance to higher professions, if desired."

Once more Numar paused to permit comment or questions, but none were forthcoming.

"This compulsory retirement," he explained, "of all those engaged in manual labor, at the age of forty, is to make room for those coming up, to do their work in the world when they are best equipped with health and physical energy to accomplish it. This will assure greater efficiency of operation, less accidents and disability and permit those past forty to enter new lives of self-development and self-enjoyment while yet young enough to receive the benefits of their labors."

"Wonderful idea but too visionary," Jeffrey Merrill, Secretary of Labor, was heard to remark.

"It will work," declared Numar, solemnly. "The poor laboring classes have been taught for centuries that this is a world of grief, poverty and torment and that their only hope was to seek their reward in heaven. Church and state must answer, hand in hand, for this crime of the ages. This New Plan of Living will bring to all classes, rich and poor, the peace and happiness, which man should have attained long, long ago."

"I hope you're right," voiced Secretary of State Woodruff, "but I doubt it."

Numar chose not to reply to his comment. Instead, he directed his attention at the President of the United States.

"And now I have come to what you human creatures will call—a most radical provision," he said, dramatically. "It concerns replacement of the Profit System by the Merit System."

A BOLT of lightning could not have struck with more unexpected and devastating force. Numar's announcement figuratively hit all directly between the eyes. They thought immediately in terms of bank balances, stocks and bonds, salaries and other sources of income.

"Now, just a minute," protested Cornelius Vanderton, financial advisor to the President. "We might go along with you on some of your other provisions—drastic as they are—but doing away with the profit system…"

"What else can you do?" demanded Numar. "You have a staggering national debt, growing yearly, now over seven hundred billions—with your citizens weighted down under inhumanly oppressive taxes and no hope in sight for generations. Your profit system, as operated, has made riches for the few at the blood cost of the many. All nations are now headed for world bankruptcy—no moneyed interests willing to take any losses or to write off these enormous debts in order to strike a new balance and arrive at some point nearer economic stability. The little man, as usual, carries the heaviest load—but big business and industry and investment are at last caught in the web of their own making. Your only escape is a wiping of the monetary slate clean before you are wiped out anyway."

"I dispute you on that," cried Mr. Vanderton. "We are admittedly in bad financial shape—but if it weren't for Russia…"

"Your economic picture has been growing worse and worse for years—without any aid from Russia or other world influence," said Numar. "Only the great national resources of the United States and a high production level have held you up. But higher and higher taxes have absorbed too much of your national income, kept your money men from reinvesting or expanding their businesses and industries, and taken so much away from the worker—or consumer—that you have seriously reduced his purchasing power and his standard of living, cutting your economic throat in two directions at once and committing financial suicide."

Mr. Vanderton sat down, muttering to himself.

"You must face this unpleasant fact as a stark truth," insisted Numar. "Human greed and unfair competition have defeated the laudable honest incentive of the Profit System and made it now necessary that Money be replaced by a Merit System wherein each human earns, by honest effort, the right to greater or less material happiness, in direct proportion as he puts forth the effort."

Mr. Vanderton bobbed up again.

"You mean—you would wipe out all currency, of every kind, all over the world?"

Numar nodded, smiling. "And all debts with it," he said. "Start in all over—on a basis of economic justice for all. The humans still unborn should never be saddled with the debts incurred by past generations. Even you, Mr. Vanderton, must admit that this is poor economy."

"Well, it's not desirable," frowned the President's financial advisor, "but it can't be helped."

"It *will* be in the future," promised Numar. "All compensation for labor and products will be made hereafter on the basis of *earned individual merit.* Products will be rated so many merit points in relation to value. The buyer then pays in the required number of his merit points to purchase what he wishes.

"Each citizen of the world is provided with a Merit Card and Merit Book in which he files 'Earned Merits' received for the work or services he renders each week or month.

"These Merit Cards, as I have said, possess buying power and may be punched by storekeepers in exchange for merchandise. Merchants then make drafts on the government each month in accordance with inventory of goods sold, and the government reimburses. The government has on deposit a merit credit up to the capacity of its entire population to produce, plus the value of natural resources in terms of the human merit system. The government's merit points thus run into the billions and it constitutes the national reservoir or bank, holding all operations in balance.

"All natural resources such as oil, coal, gold, silver and the like, should have remained the property of the people through their governments. The Constitution of the United States of the World provides that all nations are to reclaim and buy back, on this Merit System basis, all natural resources, holding them in trust for the people.

"All usury, one of the greatest curses of all time—the loaning of money at high rates of interest—is eliminated by the Merit System. Any individuals needing loans can get them from their governments on the basis of the merit capacity of the borrower over a certain length of time or that of his endorsers."

"What about private industry and private enterprise?" questioned Mr. Vanderton. "What becomes of them?"

"THEY operate as before, under the Merit System," smiled Numar. "They receive so many points in accordance with the established value of their business or industry and dispense these points in payment to labor or for purchase of raw materials or other supplies. But so-called capital as well as labor must keep these merit points in circulation since their value is in exchange for services or goods, not in hoarding."

"Getting back to natural resources for a movement," broke in Mr. Vanderton. "Many private industries have developed these natural resources in other nations at great expense. Are they then to surrender them at enormous sacrifice?"

"You do not seem to grasp," said Numar, "if all money should disappear from the world tonight, never to return, the peoples and businesses of the world would still have to get along. Man would have to invent some makeshift system, at least, of mutual service or helpfulness so he could continue to make and exchange the necessities of life for his labors.

"You cannot lose anything once it is gone. If we are all without the money system then we are no longer dealing with values set up by money. Nothing is basically taken away but one system of payment is simply replaced by another.

"Nations required to buy back their natural resources may sell or lease the continued purchase privilege of these resources to the private enterprises, formerly possessing them. But these same nations have the right to protect their own people first in the matter of their natural resources. No nation, however, shall unrightfully withhold the sale of its natural resources to any other needy country, which may desire to buy, at prices to be fixed by the International Council. Never again will timber, coal and oil barons be permitted to enter a country, buy up its natural resources, and wantonly, animated only by commercial greed, divest the land of its riches. God's bounty was intended for all men, not a favored few."

"I can tell you right now, Mr. Numar," predicted Mr. Vanderton, "you are going to run into plenty of opposition to this Plan."

Numar smiled. "Fortunately we came equipped to meet opposition," he said. "Only a few of our spaceships have landed—but I believe you witnessed quite a few more? We are well aware, from experience on many like planets, that greed and hate and desire to cling to old systems of thought and practice die hard in the human creature. But once he discovers that the New Plan of Living works—he is a changed *being* overnight."

"How long does this usually take?" asked the President's financial advisor, skeptically.

"That is something we cannot predict," said Numar. "But here is a change you will notice almost immediately. Establishment of the Merit System and a guaranteed subsistence level for all humans everywhere automatically removes all major incentive for crime since crime breeds under conditions of poor environment, poverty, feelings of inequality, inferiority, suppression, inordinate wealth in others, and the like.

"With the basic causes of crime removed, there is largely left only incentive for right conduct. Therefore, when humans still possess criminal tendencies, they will be recognized as diseased in mind and body and will be treated as mentally and physically ill. For this purpose, hospitals must be provided and these criminals segregated from one another as though afflicted with a contagious disease. Doctors and psychiatrists will then determine the cause of their abnormalities and cure them, when possible, instead of punishing."

ELLEN, immensely busy keeping pace with Numar's presentation and the side comments, took time to look up and say, fervently: "Mr. Numar, I'm glad you're here...for the first time I commence to feel as though there's still hope for this old world."

The man from another planet nodded, reassuringly. "There is—or we wouldn't be here. But there are enormous tasks ahead, as you can see. And one of them is going to have to be a reformation of the churches. It should be apparent to all thinking humans that God is not contained in anyone church or creed but is to be found in all forms of worship. Each human, hereafter, is to be freed from the bondage of religious oppression—given the absolute assurance that he will not be eternally damned through failure to exercise one belief or another—but may enjoy the Fatherhood of God through his Brotherhood to Man and receive a reward, here and now, for spiritual living—as well as the promise of finer life experience, through soul development, in the world to come."

"That's wonderful," cried Ellen, feelingly.

"Therefore," continued Numar, "all churches will be ordered to set aside their age-old, tradition-bound, out-moded sectarian creeds—and open their doors to all fellow creatures in worship of the one God—Creator of All—so that religious bigotry, hypocrisy, intolerance and oppression may be removed from this earth forever."

"There's where you're going to have your greatest opposition," declared President Ellsworth. "I have more trouble from the high pressure of some religious groups than any other influence in government."

Numar nodded. "That is because Man, on this planet, has not yet been permitted to join his Reason with his Faith. Therefore, Religion, his concept of God, has not evolved as he has enlarged his scientific knowledge of the Universe. He is still compelled to worship with blind Faith, not daring to open his eyes of Reason and see God, as the Infinite Father of this Unfathomable Universe really is. The clergy is afraid it will lose its hold on man if man thinks for himself when it comes to Religion. Therefore these devout men of God, many of them as blind as the followers they lead, cling to old religious ceremonies, rituals and spiritual concepts based upon early mythology or superstition when the Great God of Creation is all about them—in and of all things—ready to reveal a power and glory in the hearts and minds of man, once enlightened and freed from the shackles of narrow, prejudiced doctrines—which will fill all churches to overflowing and lead to the long sought brotherhood of all races."

Andy, face illumined, was impelled to cry out: "You have the answer, Mister Numar—but will humans accept it? Think of all the different, conflicting religions on this Earth. The Christian, the Jewish, Mohammedan, Persian, Hindu, Moslem,

Buddhism, Shintoism and so on and on...how can they all be reconciled and brought under one religious banner of worship to the one God, over all?"

"It will take time," said Numar, "but education of the masses in every country will give them the power to think and act, unfettered by the fear of eternal punishment or damnation. All humans will then gradually enlarge their concepts, develop more tolerance for the viewpoints of others and come to realize, as a combined Faith and Reason experience, that God is the One Great Reality in All Things and that each human is actually a Divine Spark, united to all other humans as a Mighty Flame. These humans are capable, once banded together in Brotherhood, of achieving a real heaven on Earth, as the Great Intelligence had originally intended when Man was given Free Will and then, unhappily, abused this finest of all gifts."

NUMAR'S remarks were too thought provoking to elicit much comment or discussion. Not a word of protest or opinion had been volunteered by the Secretaries of War, Navy and Aviation. They had sat in a little, unspeaking group—their minds, geared to military problems and objectives—hardest hit by this Plan of Living, which left no room for their operations.

"The function of government should obviously be to serve the people, not to tyrannize," Numar declared, veering to a different phase of his subject. "But this function exists in theory more than fact. Take your own United States government for example. You gentlemen, in political office, serve that section of American citizens who are best organized to maintain powerful lobbies in Washington or stir up the greatest amount of agitation in your home districts. Other groups of Americans, equally deserving but not so organized, whose voting power you do not fear—receive little or no consideration from you. Is this fair dealing? Are you not constantly exploiting your fellow humans to further your own personal ends? Do you not admit that favoritism, prejudice and special privilege exist on every side?

"This condition is not only true of government—it is true of your laws and your courts, especially as they concern divorce, control of traffic and punishment of crime.

"Humanity is weighed down and overburdened with useless, involved, overlapping senseless, outmoded laws. One of the provisions in the Constitution of the United States of the World will call for the elimination, simplification and standardization of divorce, traffic and crime laws, among others—to the end that equal justice maybe administered to all in all nations.

"Under the Merit System, money can no longer buy a judge, fix a jury or ruin the reputation of an honest man by deliberate smear campaigns. Each human, of whatever race or color, will be on his own—charged with the responsibility to do his job in the world, assured that he will be rewarded as he serves. Today there is no guarantee of such reward but, rather, the almost moral certainty that, unless an individual belongs to a powerful trades union or some equally influential organization, he may not even be permitted to work in this supposedly free America. The price tag is upon everything. Without the price in money or connections, the human suffers, often to the point of deprivation.

"Do you wonder, gentlemen, now that you reflect upon it, that you are facing growing unrest among increasing masses in your own population? All because you permitted organized groups, bringing pressure upon you, to secure special privileges. More and more your government of the United States of America has shifted from a government 'of the people, by the people and for the people' to a government 'by the few for the benefit of the few—at the expense of the many.'"

Numar's paraphrasing accusation hit home with paralyzing force. If there was a time when he should have been challenged, it was now—but no governmental official dared to take issue with him. They could tell that he was too well equipped with the facts—such facts as would embarrass and confound them in debate. The safest procedure was to discuss a less explosive phase of Numar's comments, which Mr. Vanderton elected to do.

"Mister Numar," he addressed him, "you spoke of this compulsory retirement provision at the age of forty for all humans who have worked at a trade or at physical labor. But how about the executives, the brainworkers of the world, the men and women who supply the ideas, which make the wheels of the world go around? What becomes of them?"

NUMAR smiled. "Higher Merit Ratings are given in recognition of developed executive, creative or inventive ability," he said, "and opportunity for indefinite active service is granted beyond the bounds of the minimum basic requirements, as such individuals demonstrate these skills, at whatever age."

"That's encouraging," said the President's financial advisor, with an attempted flash of humor. "I don't feel quite like sitting on the sidelines as yet." Then he grew more serious. "But this guarantee of subsistence you speak of, Mister Numar. How is it to be administered?"

"When applied for and as needed," answered Numar, instantly. "As soon as the Merit System is installed the government will have a complete census of the needs of all its citizens. Each citizen, existing on subsistence, will be required to give the government four hours service daily, if physically or mentally able and, when gainfully employed, will make reimbursement for the subsistence as rendered, if it is adjudged humanly possible. After the age of forty, when full service has been rendered, either in private or government employment, every citizen receives a special Merit Bonus and is entitled to subsistence support, if needed, for the balance of life—also free access to all schools and courses of study—as well as admission to special entertainments and lectures and musicales at special Merit Point rates. This is the time of life for which the first Forty Years of service have been lived—when Man is to reap his reward and more deeply and fully experience the joys this Earth has to offer, instead of ending his days in poverty, despair and ill health."

"It's a beautiful picture," admitted Mr. Vanderton, "but the life insurance companies won't like it."

This brought the first resounding laugh of the session, there being no life insurance agents present.

"When the automobile arrived on your planet, the horse and buggy disappeared," said Numar. "Life insurance, up to the present time, has provided the only feeling of security that millions of humans have ever had. And yet, millions of others, even more direly in need of such security, have not been reached by life insurance at all because they could not afford it. Your government and other governments have been criminally liable in gross neglect of their citizens who have been allowed to exist in conditions of unspeakable poverty, ill health and misery, touched now and then by the hand of charity but never given such support as would have placed them on their feet and restored them to self-respecting, nourished, healthy, happy members of their own community.

"These humans have been the victims of a faulty economy, an indifferent government, and the willingness of organized religions to call their plight 'the will of God.'

"Let those who would deny such accusations offer proof to the contrary," concluded Numar, as a murmuring protest was heard.

IT WAS past four in the morning and approaching time for the next rising of the sun. Numar called attention to the fact that the Great Light was waning.

"It is being withdrawn," he informed, to the quite apparent relief of those present. "If the peoples on this planet respond as they should to the New Plan of Living, it may not be necessary for the Light to return."

"Let's hope they do," said President Ellsworth. "I don't believe I could stand another night like this."

"I will not hold you much longer," said Numar, "I have merely sketched some of the outstanding features and provisions of this Constitution to give you a little glimpse of the changes you may expect. The management of this World Government is to be placed in the hands of a Council of Sixteen, to be appointed by me. I have chosen sixteen young men, all under the age of thirty-five, with minds still fresh and pliable—one each from the embassies here in Washington, of England, France, Germany, Italy, Netherlands, Egypt, Africa, India, Asia, Russia, China, Japan, Australia, South America, Canada—and your own State Department. These young diplomatic representatives, whose real names I will later announce, will serve under my direction in the administration of this Plan, issuing orders to the rulers of all countries for their governing bodies and their people to carry out."

This pronouncement brought a raising of eyebrows and an exchange of consulting glances.

"This Council of Sixteen is to be supplemented by a Council of All Other Nations," Numar continued, "with power to recommend but not to control. All power is left in the hands of the nations who dominate the commerce of the world and whose basic co-operation is essential to economic stability, even on the Merit System. The nations, above mentioned, because of their power and influence, have been most responsible for the condition the world is now in.

"You have an old saying on your planet: 'To whom much is given, from them much is expected.' The rule of these sixteen nations will not alienate the rights of smaller nations—since the citizens of all countries, large and small, are guaranteed their basic individual freedoms."

Numar paused that he might stress what he termed as a most important point.

"You, in the United States, have been eager to force acceptance of the Democratic Way of Life upon peoples in foreign lands," he said. "Your intentions have been good but your psychological understanding of other peoples has been woefully misguided. I tell you now that many humans on this planet are not yet progressed in education and self-discipline to the point of being ready for self-government and must thus be governed, for the time being, in the manner to which they have been accustomed, *except* as freedom from oppression is instantly conferred upon them, together with provision for basic subsistence, as an inherent, God-given right of all humans, everywhere."

NUMAR once more took time to let his remarks soak in. While he was doing so, Secretary of State Woodruff addressed him.

"Mister Numar, this Plan you have outlined is too colossal and far-reaching for any of us to intelligently pass upon without a great deal of study—and maybe, even then, we'd learn more about it, in operation, than we ever could arguing about it. But I'd like to ask—is there any new governing body to be set up in the individual nations, outside of the one here in Washington, you've just described?"

"Yes," said Numar. "Each nation maintains, as you know, ambassadors or consuls or government representatives of some sort, in all other countries. My Leaders in these countries are now preparing to set up duplicate organizations—a Council of Sixteen and a supplementary Council of All Other Nations, with membership comprised of young men and women, under thirty-five, selected from the diplomatic corps of the different countries, now in service.

"The members of these Councils will function as 'clearing houses' for the interchange of all relations between their respective nations as they concern the country in which they are residing.

"They will meet, each day, for as long as is required to dispose of urgent matters having to do with international affairs. Today, embassies and consulates operate largely independently and nonco-operatively—each looking out for its own nation's interests in foreign lands—bound around and bogged down by governmental formality, red tape and secret diplomacy.

"This is all to be changed and, when English becomes the Universal Language, all translations will be dispensed with and greater understanding with more effective co-operation will be possible.

"There will be no secret conferences. Each session of any Council, anywhere, will be open to the public and broadcast so that citizens of the world may know how their interests are being represented, at all times.

"Thus, any difficulties arising anywhere on earth can be acted upon by representative bodies at the scene, who will forward their reports and recommendations to the Master Council of Sixteen in Washington whose decisions are final."

Secretary of State Woodruff waved his hand.

"A question?" smiled Numar.

"Yes, under this Plan of procedure—what would happen to our State Department?"

"It would be more active than ever before—maintaining a worldwide staff of young men and women—especially trained and qualified for this important diplomatic service," explained Numar. "Your own authority would be greatly curtailed since the member of the Council of Sixteen, from your Department, would be empowered to act for the United States on all international matters."

"I see," said Secretary of State Woodruff, with little genuine warmth.

"AS FOR the President of the United States, and the rulers of all other nations," continued Numar, "they would concern themselves, hereafter, with the conduct and administration of domestic affairs—seeing to it that their respective countries are run in the most efficient and harmonious manner possible. Each ruler is to serve for one term of six years only, irrespective of the form of government, so that new minds with fresh outlooks may carryon the destiny of each nation as it grows and develops and prospers as a member of the family of nations."

"It is a great governmental fallacy to believe that any one human is indispensable.

"However, in the future, no public office can be occupied in any country except by those carefully trained and educated for the positions they seek.

"No business man could ever elect any man or woman to an important executive position in his company unless he or she were thoroughly experienced and qualified to render competent service. It is a miracle that the vastly more important big business of government has survived this long on the patronage system of rewarding incompetent, often corrupt 'party faithfuls' to important offices for which they have had no training or education."

This was a last final blow against, which all assembled, were entirely defenseless.

The man from another planet now took, from beneath his white robe, a thick appearing document and placed it on the table in front of President Ellsworth.

"Here, Mister President, is an exact copy of the Constitution for the United States of the world," he said. "I am returning to my space ship but will be back later in the day, at which time I expect this Constitution to have been approved by your legislative bodies and by the other governments as well. For the present then, I bid you a pleasant good morning."

Numar strode toward the door and all in the room rose to their feet.

"My car is outside," said the President. "Let me see you to it."

"Thank you," smiled Numar, bowing. "You are very kind."

He and the President went out together. The door had scarcely closed on them than a pandemonium of comment and discussion burst with tornado force.

"It will never work!"

"Our people won't accept it!"

"There'll be world revolution!"

"We might as well blow the planet up and be done with it!"

"Imagine being criticized like this by someone who doesn't even belong on this earth!"

"I still think it's a plot to enslave us all and to take over this planet!"

"But what are we going to do? This Numar and his forces are too powerful!"

A PERSPIRING President Ellsworth, returning, put an end to wild talk and speculation. As all looked to their Chief Executive for some suggested way out of this seemingly unsolvable predicament, the only comment he could offer was a helpless: "Charming gentleman, isn't he?"

"Charming, my eye!" blazed Secretary of War Wade. "I'm for destroying his space ship with him in it—and taking our chances against a shooting war with the invaders!"

President Ellsworth shook his head, decisively.

"No, Henry," he said, "we still need a planet to live on. You'll notice the Great Light has disappeared and that's the glorious old sun coming up out there. We're adjourning now for breakfast—that is, if any of you can eat after this. Then, when we get back, I'm calling a joint session of both houses of Congress and reading this Constitution to them. We'll have to devise ways and means of rushing it through both bodies—what a headache, when it's taken months to put ordinary legislation through now. But we've got to do it, gentlemen, like it or not—there can't be any sleep or peace for us, till we do."

CHAPTER TWELVE

A SLEEPLESS world, dazed and still frightened by events, but relieved that the mysterious and terrorizing Great Light had disappeared, tried to collect its senses as it entered upon the second twenty-four hour period since these strange happenings began.

No news had yet been given out on the meetings taking place at all national capitals between the countries' rulers and the Talamayan Leaders, acting under orders from their Commander-in-Chief Numar—who had landed at Washington, D. C.

Few humans could rest until some word was received as to what their fate might be. Newspaper offices, radio stations and government bureaus were overwhelmed with hysterical calls but could only answer that they had not yet been advised. A mad rumor raced through highly emotional Europe that all rulers and their governing bodies had been killed and that these powerful Green Men had taken over the governments. Thousands of frantic humans sought to defend themselves to the death as best they could with weapons concealed at home, until their fears were allayed by government statements that their rulers were "still in conference."

Ellen and Andy, weary in body and mind, were too excited to sleep and talked over cups of coffee in a little "hole in the wall" restaurant not far from the White House. Ellen knew the proprietor, Old Mac McKinley, proud distant descendant of a one-time President of the United States.

"You're in on every thin', Miss Hopper," he said, as he served them. "What's happenin'? Did you see the Green Monster?"

"Been talking to him," said Ellen. "He's not a monster."

"Not human, either, I've heard folks say. Strange bein' of some sort. I saw him pass by in the car with the President last night. Was it last night? Bright as day, anyway. And will that Great Light come again, did he say? My little granddaughter cried and screamed all the time. Her mother had to take her in a dark closet and line the bottom of the door, along the crack, with an old dress, to keep the light out...she finally rocked little Anna to sleep in there. Pretty terrible thing to frighten people all over the world that way. What's goin' to become of us?"

Ellen smiled, as reassuringly as she could.

"I don't know, Mr. Mac. Things are pretty serious. They were even before the Green Man came."

"He told us to take a three-day holiday," said Old Mac. "I couldn't do that...got my regular customers to take care of come end of the world or not."

"Don't worry, Mac," said Andy, eager to talk to Ellen alone. "As soon as we learn what this is all about, we'll let you know. They'll announce it on the radio and in the papers before the day's over…take it easy."

Old Mac turned from their table.

"Shouldn't frighten people this way," he repeated, shaking his head. "It's no good…no good."

Ellen and Andy, drawing deep breaths, looked at one another.

"Whew," said Ellen. "Pinch me. Is this really happening?"

"It's happening all right," said Andy. "This is no illusion. It's one prophecy that came true. But what do you make of it? Numar—I mean?"

Ellen hesitated. "I'd rather you'd express your opinion first."

Andy thought for a moment. "If I had ever met a God," he said, slowly, "I would say he was close to one—in comparison, that is, to us humans. Of course—I've never visualized a God as being *green.*"

"Nor I," laughed Ellen. "Numar's obviously far, far beyond us in body form and intellect. If he's actually existed for some millions of years—just this immensity of time would have given him experiences and wisdom we can't even comprehend."

"Exactly," said Andy. "His knowledge of us and our planet alone is simply stupendous…down to personal incidents and details. He speaks our English language as though it were his native tongue and I had the feeling, several times, that he was deliberately simplifying everything he said and did to make himself appear as close to human as he could."

"That was my observation, too," checked Ellen. "No wonder Mother was impressed with Numar when she saw him years ago. You wouldn't forget such a personage—ever. I know I never shall. I'll probably be telling about this to my grandchildren, too."

Andy reached over to press her hand. "Couldn't it possibly be—our grandchildren?" he whispered.

"You pick the strangest times to propose," smiled Ellen. "Try me again some time when we're not on the verge of a war with Russia—or an invasion from space. I feel about as romantic now as a kernel of popcorn in a popper!"

ANDY was amused at himself. "I'll try to do better next time," he promised, "but don't forget, meanwhile, that I have my bid in."

Their eyes met and Ellen looked away. "I wonder what Russia is thinking about all this?" she said, suddenly, changing the subject.

"You mean," corrected Andy, sobering, "that you wonder what Petrov Gouchevisky is thinking."

Ellen's face colored. "Well, he's Russian...yes. What do you suppose he is thinking?"

"Unless he's had a report from his government on the results of their conference, not having sat in on ours, I doubt if he's thinking much at all," said Andy, a bit sharply. "We're privileged people—at the moment. We know as much as can be known—which isn't too much."

"Then let me ask you," said Ellen, pointedly. "What do you think of Mister Numar's Plan?"

Andy looked off into space. "I went on record that I would support it before he had presented it," he reflected. "I'm still not sorry I did it. But I'll say this—if we humans, at this stage of our development proposed such a plan—or if any country, the United States or Russia sought to impose it on the world—we'd be considered mad."

"Do you think Numar is mad?" asked Ellen.

"No—but I think he's some thousands of years ahead of his time for this earth," said Andy. "We may evolve into these ideas and practices eventually—but to establish them overnight—or even in a few years—well, the forces of opposition are just too great."

"They would be for us," admitted Ellen. "But Numar quite evidently knows that—and this is why he's made such a display of his own power—to subdue these forces at the outset."

"That's not so easy," said Andy, with the wisdom of his few intensive years in the State Department. "They will use every device, every subterfuge, every trick and strategy to delay, obstruct and defeat the working of any Plan, designed for the good of the world, which is inimical to their interests."

"I'm willing to predict they've met their match in Mister Numar," said Ellen. "I, somehow, have tremendous confidence in Mother's Green Man. He's apparently no novice at this sort of thing. He indicated that he's put other planets of human creatures on their feet. He may have to treat 'em rough, but I'll bet he'll get results."

"He'll *have* to treat 'em rough," said Andy. "Millions of humans today are so downtrodden and disheartened that they just won't make the effort to lift themselves up unless kicked from behind."

"It's not a kick they need," differed Ellen. "It's a lift from *within* that I think Numar's going to give them. Andy, you wait and see—I've a hunch of my own. I think you and I are alive in what is going to be the greatest, most exciting time on this earth."

"Come on," said Andy. "We'd better be getting over to the Capitol Building. If that's true we don't want to miss anything—and this specially called session of both Houses of Congress ought to be worth going miles to see."

BY EARLY afternoon the sensational session of the United States Congress and its capitulation to the demands of Numar, self-styled Liberator from the Planet of Talamaya, was world news. Reports coming in from all other countries were of the same nature. England capitulates, France capitulates, Germany capitulates...Russia capitulates!

President Ellsworth went on the air in a nationwide radio broadcast, which was short-waved and televised, to all parts of the world.

"And so," he concluded, "we have placed ourselves, as a Nation, in the hands of Mr. Numar and his host of Green Men from the far-off planet of Talamaya, promising to give him every co-operation as he and his associates prepare to put their New Plan of Living into operation on this Earth.

"So that the citizens of my country and the peoples of the world may clearly understand why we have taken this unprecedented step, I would like to frankly state that, after due deliberation, we determined that we had no choice but to accede to the stipulations laid down for us.

"Those who have taken the affairs of this planet in charge made it plain that it was either our complete annihilation or our cooperation—the decision was up to us.

"The Constitution for the United States of the World is being published in every newspaper in all countries within the next twenty-four hours. I beg every individual everywhere to not only read it—but study it—for you will be compelled to live up to the new laws and practices herein set forth to the best of your ability and capacity.

"You may expect, from this time on, great new changes in government and in everyday living to commence to take place. The provisions of this Constitution will be put into effect as soon as the foundation can be laid for them.

"And now—all networks are to be silenced so that Mister Numar, himself, can speak to the world from his space ship at the Municipal Airport here in Washington, D. C. His message will be translated immediately afterward, by his own Leaders in the various foreign countries and repeated by them to the peoples there, in their native tongue.

"Mr. Numar's talk will be beamed to the world by a technique that we cannot comprehend. You will hear him as you did upon his arrival, seemingly speaking to you as though he were right beside you.

"One word more—do not fear the new phenomena you may observe, from time to time. We believe that Mister Numar and his associates are here to help us find a better way of life—if we can. I've pledged the co-operation of every citizen of the United States to this end—and I urge you to do your part in fulfilling this pledge."

A radio announcer cut in, speaking rapidly.

"You've just heard Norman Ellsworth, President of the United States, ladies and gentlemen, delivering a special broadcast message in this most critical hour in the world's history. This network now leaves the air with all other networks to make way for Mister Numar, New Head of All Governments on this Earth, who is about to speak…"

Almost instantly the Voice of the man from another planet started speaking—out of the atmosphere, seemingly—indoors or outdoors—it made no difference—in even-volumed, mellow-sounding, friendly tones.

"Greetings—all peoples of Earth!

"The Great Change has begun to take place on your planet.

"From this moment on, you are all citizens of the United States of the World, bound by a Constitution, which guarantees you freedom from want and oppression.

"Each of your governments, in extraordinary sessions assembled, have ratified this Constitution, which automatically cancels any laws or customs or provisions heretofore existing anywhere, which may have been in conflict.

"Your newspapers and radio announcers will keep you informed of all details.

"It will require three months of your time to put this New Plan of Living in full operation.

"Your Rulers have agreed to obey all orders as given by me, the Director General of this Plan—as well as all orders issued by the Council of Sixteen, which I am herewith appointing. This Council to have complete control of all International Affairs.

"Young men and women, under thirty-five years of age, will comprise this Council. In the present state of your world, too many minds of older men and women in high positions of public trust have developed fixed ideas, prejudices and hates, which have totally unfitted them for dealing fairly and impartially with those complex problems existing between nations.

"I have chosen the Council of Sixteen from the Embassy staffs of the sixteen nations, which wield the most influence in your world today. These young men and women have all had experience in international relations and are the best available. In time to come, graduates of the School for International Co-operation will take their places.

"In no public office, anywhere on earth, may any official, however praiseworthy his service, remain longer than six years. He may pass on to other duties and positions but still pools of water stagnate and running streams are everlastingly fresh and pure.

"Everything in nature is changing, evolving from lower to higher forms. You humans must no longer stand in the way of your own upward progress. And you must train other humans to take your places so that you have nations of leaders rather than followers.

"Know today that you are free to think and speak and write and act as you choose, within the laws of decency and right conduct.

"To be free, you must first let others be free. Therefore, true freedom means a freeing of your mind from all previous racial, religious and political prejudices and hatreds—accepting every man as your brother. This is an absolute requirement of the New Plan of Living, which will soon be functioning on this Earth.

"The State, your Government, is your Servant. You are no longer a vassal. You are responsible citizens of this State—and of the Union of States—which make up your World.

"Freedom does not mean Free License. You will be governed by Laws and compelled to do your part in the family of nations.

"You must pay the price for this new freedom bestowed upon you—by service to your community, your State and to the world.

"Obey, without question, the orders of your Rulers and myself. Until you have grown in wisdom and experience, you must rely upon those who possess such knowledge. Your guarantee that your confidence is not misplaced is in the freedom already extended.

"In due course of time, when you have learned how to govern and discipline yourselves in this New Freedom, all over-control will be withdrawn.

"May God speed this day!"

ELLEN and Andy were just two of the two and a half billions held spellbound by this address of Numar's, which was translated into all tongues, as he spoke, and delivered in all countries by his Leaders there.

But their greatest thrill was yet to come—for Numar, in listing the names of those chosen by him to serve on the Council of Sixteen—held his appointments for the world's two most powerful nations to the last, and then said:

"...representing Russia, Mr. Petrov Gouchevisky...and the United States of America, Mr. Andrew Brownell..."

Ellen and Andy were on the Capitol steps where an immense crowd had gathered to hear the President and Ellen, at Numar's announcement, cried out, joyously: "Oh, Andy—I could kiss you—if it wasn't for all these people. Such an honor. I'm so happy for you! Petrov, too!"

"Petrov, too," repeated Andy, in a low voice. "Always Petrov."

"Two of the finest men who ever represented their countries," whispered Ellen. "Believe me, Andy. And to think you don't have to play this secret diplomatic game any longer. You can meet, as fair-minded men, and put everything right on the table. No governments or selfish interests can force you to do things you know aren't just—because Numar and his powers won't let them. Oh, it's too wonderful to even think about. I must phone Petrov and congratulate him, too. Russia isn't our enemy any longer—she's a co-operator, with us, for the kind of decent world we've all really wanted."

Ellen hadn't intended such an outburst. She found herself clutching Andy's arm with both hands, her head resting against his shoulder, lips close to his ear. Government officials, nearby, sighting Andy, were pushing through to him.

"Ssssh, Ellen," warned Andy. "I hope all you say is true. I'm too dazed right at this moment to figure anything out. We're too conspicuous here. Let's get into the Capitol building before this crowd recognizes us. This appointment will spotlight me—make me one of the most marked men in the world—and that's not so good."

Andy was leading Ellen up the steps toward the Capitol entrance. They had been in a little reserved section and guards, knowing Andy, now commenced clearing away for him. But a pageboy, sighting him, began calling.

"Mr. Brownell! Oh, Mr., Brownell!"

"Yes, sonny, what is it?" called Andy.

"The President requests your presence at once—in the President's room," said the boy.

"Coming right away," said Andy, as secret service men formed around him. "You see, Ellen," he pointed out, "my life's not my own from now on. This is one of the toughest assignments ever handed a human being."

"Won't it be just as tough for Petrov?" rejoined Ellen.

"For all sixteen," said Andy. "But toughest for Petrov and myself—because we represent the two biggest powers on earth. Why do you suppose the President is sending for me?"

"Why—why to congratulate you, of course," said Ellen.

Andy laughed. "Yes, he'll do that—but he'll have instructions—so will everyone else. Numar's Plan may be wonderful but, the minute he tries to put it in operation, he's bucking *human nature.*"

They were walking along the marble corridor now, inside a small phalanx of Capitol guards.

"Are you sorry you were chosen?" asked Ellen, disturbed at Andy's reaction.

"No," he said, grimly. "I practically asked for it, but I know what I'm up against. We've escaped man-made atomic bombs but now we're facing something just as devastating—man's age-old resistance to change."

THEY had reached the entrance to the President's Room, just off the Senate Chamber. Ellen stopped, releasing her hold on Andy's arm. She gave his shoulder a little reassuring, parting pat.

"Let's hope it won't be as bad as you think," she said. "Don't forget—you're not in this fight alone—you have a power greater than human on your side."

Andy smiled. "Without that," he said, "there wouldn't be any hope at all." He bent over quickly and kissed her on the cheek. "Wait for me here—do you mind?"

Ellen nodded, face flushed. "Sir!" she said.

CHAPTER THIRTEEN

NUMAR'S appointment of the State Department's ace troubleshooter, Secretary of State Woodruff's white-haired boy, to represent his country on the Council of Sixteen in charge of International Affairs had, in human phraseology, "kicked him upstairs" in authority over every other official, including the President.

When Andrew Brownell walked into the President's Room on a summons from his Chief Executive, he carried with him more power than any other American citizen had ever possessed. Hastily assembled to meet him were all Cabinet members and high-ranking officials of other Departments. There was an air of great excitement and concern.

"We want you to know, Mr. Brownell," spoke President Ellsworth, looking near collapse as a result of no sleep and the exhausting day, "that we are delighted with Mister Numar's choice of you for this post. The fact that you knew of him through Miss Hopper and her mother no doubt has created a personal interest in him for you. At least—this is what we are banking on—that, if he is partial to any human—that human should be *you*. In that case you may be able to influence him. I mean—work things out so that the interests of our country are protected, and any changes instituted will favor the United States."

Andy stood facing the President. He had been given little time to orient himself but his mind was commencing to function in the new and wider channel created for it by this authoritative position.

"I very much doubt, Mr. President and gentlemen," Andy heard himself replying, "that I can wield any special influence with Mister Numar. And, if I could, I am frank to state that I would not."

Secretary of State Woodruff jumped to his feet, eyes blazing.

"Then what kind of a representative of our country are you?" he fired.

"Let me answer that," shot back Andy, "by asking whether you wish Mr. Numar's New Plan of Living to succeed or fail? Are you suggesting that I begin my service with this Council of Sixteen by endeavoring to sabotage it through seeking favors for my own country?"

"What do you think the other fifteen members will be doing?" countered Woodruff.

"I can only speak for myself," said Andy. "I intend to co-operate fully and honestly with my fellow members, under Mister Numar's guidance. All human plans for world peace and happiness have failed. As I view it, we are being given a last chance here, through Mister Numar's intervention on our behalf. Therefore, gentlemen, you must not try to compromise me. I must be free to think and act for the good of all countries, believing if I do that, we will derive the greatest benefit ourselves."

A nervous President Ellsworth interrupted.

"That's all very well, Mr. Brownell. Extremely laudable and all that. But our big business interests, industrialists and bankers have been after us all day—wanting to know what to expect of the future. They tell me—were it not for this three-day holiday, the stock market would have gone down out of sight. They're afraid to let it re-open after reading this World Constitution, which plans to do away with money. We weren't in position to tell Mister Numar so—but that's a crackpot idea, if there ever was one. Nothing will bring the world to ruin quicker than to eliminate the Profit System and introduce a Merit System. It's up to you to make Mr. Numar see this—get the support of other members of the Council—get Numar to change his Plan!"

THE State Department's white-haired boy could feel some real white hairs coming.

"Mr. President," he said, "you know, as well as I, and every gentleman in this room—that I can't hope to influence Mister Numar to that extent, if at all. This Plan of Living has apparently been tested and proved on other planets and Numar has come here with sufficient threat of force to see that we try it out, whether we like it or not."

General Wade, Secretary of War, stood up and shook his fist. "Then, by God—I still say we should fight—regardless of the odds—and go down that way—instead of submitting spinelessly to this humiliation!"

"I don't know," said Andy, surprised at his own defiance, "there's just a bare possibility that the Plan, properly enforced and directed, might work—and, if it did, it will beat anything we humans have been able to develop since we supposedly became civilized."

This statement brought a torrent of protests.

"I can see now," charged Secretary of State Woodruff, "that we are going to get no help from our representative on the

Council. It is regrettable that we have no power to remove him. Asinine, too, that only young persons under thirty-five are permitted to serve. It takes years of experience in the field to be a good diplomat. I was grooming Mr. Brownell for big things years hence, giving him more and more authority—but it's quite evident that this appointment by a Being from Another Planet has gone to his head!"

Andy smiled. "You would have been pleased, no doubt, to have been appointed in my stead?" he replied.

"Well, I...er...would certainly not sell out my country," sputtered Secretary of State Woodruff, "which it is obvious you are preparing to do."

Andy, stung by this charge, retorted, hotly, "That's not true, and you know it! But there have been many things in our foreign relations, which haven't been honest and above-board— as there are with all nations. If I try to carry them over into this new set-up, then it becomes corrupted, too. But this I refuse to do. You forget, gentlemen, that you are no longer just the United States of America—you are *a* State in the United States of the *World!*"

President Ellsworth gave out a great groan of helplessness and placed hands to a throbbing head.

"Session adjourned," he said. "Come on, gentlemen, let's get home and get to bed. The world can go to hell if it wants to. I can't take any more."

ELLEN, left to herself with time on her hands, went in search of a telephone booth. Finding one, she called the Russian Embassy on a hunch that Petrov Gouchevisky would be there.

"Who wants him?" asked a man's voice.

"A personal friend," she said.

"Give your name, please," the voice insisted.

"Miss Hopper," said Ellen.

"Just a moment. I believe Mr. Gouchevisky is in conference. Hold the wire."

Ellen waited. She felt suddenly nervous and depleted. It had been one terrific day and night—a gigantic strain on all humans everywhere. But she had been in the center of activities—had enjoyed a ringside seat at the drama of the ages—and it wasn't over yet. She brushed back dark wisps of hair, which fell, over her eyes.

"I don't dare look at myself in a mirror," she thought, with a little tremor of horror. "I must be a sight."

"Hello," said the voice. "Mr. Gouchevisky will be with you. Hold on, please."

Ellen held, and the minutes ticked off. She could finally hear excited voices in Russian, an argument of some kind. Apparently Petrov's appointment to the Council of Sixteen had caused a stir among his Russian associates, too. Ellen thought of what Andy had said about being placed under pressure from all sides. This was never easy… It would be incomparably more trying with this unprecedented state of affairs now.

"Hello." It was Petrov's voice, worn and disturbed. "Miss Hopper? Sorry to keep you waiting all this while but I…"

"Oh, Pete, that's all right. I know you must be terribly busy—but I just had to phone and tell you how glad I am you've been chosen on the Council," cried Ellen. "I just feel— with men like Andy—I mean, Mr. Brownell—and you—well, working together instead of against each other there's got to be a better world."

"It's too early yet to tell," was Petrov's cautious reply. "I have not met this Green Man. It is all very confusing at the moment. But I appreciate your calling, Miss Hopper…thank you very much."

It was evident that Petrov was where he could not talk. He was even afraid of what Ellen might stay at her end of the line. But she decided she would risk one comment, anyway.

"You'll like Mister Numar, Peter. He's pretty super, all right, but there's something close to human about him."

"Have you met him?" There was a pick-up in Petrov's voice.

"Met him," repeated Ellen. "I've been *with* him, off and on, since he arrived."

She could feel an electric wave of interest reach out to her over the wire. Had she said something that she shouldn't? No—there wasn't to be any more secret diplomacy. It didn't matter if he knew that she knew Mr. Numar. He would be meeting him soon, himself.

"You don't mean—you weren't present at the Conference?" asked Petrov, unbelievingly.

"Yes—yes, I *was*," cried Ellen.

"But you were fired from the White House," said Petrov. "I don't understand."

Ellen laughed. "Oh, Peter...I'd forgotten. Things have been happening so fast. No, everything's forgiven now...you see, my mother...maybe you read about it in the paper...she met Mister Numar years ago on his first trip to this planet. And I, naturally...oh, it's too long a story to tell over the phone...but, anyway, I was called in to take notes on the meeting. It was mostly all about the World Constitution...but it was thrilling to hear Mister Numar tell about it."

"He came direct to the United States and not to Russia," said Petrov. "Moscow is naturally suspicious."

ELLEN gasped. "Well, he had to come—either to one country or the other. I suppose if he had landed in Moscow and conferred with your government first, *we'd* have been suspicious. But I assure you, Pete—there's no favoritism being shown. In fact, Mister Numar criticized us severely as he did the conduct of all other countries. You tell Moscow you have it on good authority that there's no collusion. This whole development is on the level—it's out of all human hands—and Mister Numar just can't be influenced by any individual or nation."

There was a moment's silence on the wire and a background of voices in Russian.

"Thank you, Miss Hopper," said Petrov, finally. "What you have told me is very interesting. I will have to get in touch with you later. Good-bye for now."

He hung up, quickly, as was his habit—but Ellen could sense, this time, that the entire Russian Embassy was in a turmoil of perplexity and indecision.

Andy was still seething inside when he emerged from the President's Room in the spot in the corridor where Ellen was waiting.

"Things go as you expected?" she asked. Then, quickly, "You don't need to answer—I can see that they did."

Andy took her arm and piloted her out a side entrance. Secret service men were following at a respectful distance.

"I'm taking you home," he announced. "I'm practically walking in my sleep. You'd better get some rest, too, or we'll both be wrecks by tomorrow. Mister Numar's apt to call the first Council meeting by then, and I want to be fresh for that."

"How disappointing. I expected dinner and the theatre," said Ellen, as they hailed a cab and got in. Both relaxed and laughed as they slumped against each other.

They rode some blocks, without speaking, then Ellen ventured: "Andy—I talked with Petrov."

Fatigued as he was, Andy sat up and eyed her.

"You did? Where? How?"

"By phone, Silly. He was at the Embassy—and, if it's any consolation to you, he was having his troubles, too. I think, along the same order."

"What did you say to him?" Andy demanded.

"Why, nothing much. Just offered my congratulations. Said I thought it would be fine for you two to be working together...and that I was much impressed by Mister Numar."

Andy leaned back. "Is that all?"

"Just about. Why? Is there anything I shouldn't have said?"

Andy smiled, wearily. "I guess not—just so you didn't tell him that you loved him."

His head dropped back—and a slight snore escaped his lips.

THE cab pulled up outside Ellen's apartment house. She slipped quietly from the taxi and, placing fingers to her lips, said in a low voice: "Driver, please take this gentleman to his home at One Hundred Washington Place. He's not drunk—he's just asleep."

"Okay, Miss," grinned the red-eyed cabbie. "I'm apt to be asleep myself before I get there."

When she turned her key in the lock, Ellen had the uncanny feeling that there was someone in her apartment. She opened the door, cautiously. It was late afternoon—almost dinnertime—and there was the unmistakable odor of food cooking in her kitchen.

"Who's there?" she cried.

A bright-faced elderly woman appeared in the kitchen doorway, wearing her apron, stirring spoon in hand.

"Mother!" shrieked Ellen. "How'd *you* get here?"

"Flew," said Grandma Hopper. "Came to see the Green Man. You weren't here so I got the desk clerk to let me in. I remembered you were always hungry the minute you got home, and you had plenty of food on hand…"

Ellen bounded across the room and hugged her mother. "You dear old witch, you! What a surprise!"

"What a *day,*" beamed Mrs. Hopper. "Have you met Mister Numar yet—and what do you think of him? We're going to have a real world at last, Ellen—and I'm going to live to see it! Praises be! I just couldn't wait to get here. I told Harry to use his influence and throw anybody off a plane, if he had to, and get me on. But most folks are scared to fly now—they think the Green Men are going to shoot 'em down out of the skies. Pshaw, they don't know Mister Numar. I've been telling everybody…"

"Mother. *Mother!*" cried Ellen, shaking her, good-naturedly. "Stop. Catch your breath and let me catch mine… I'm dog-tired, I don't know whether I can eat or not. I just want to drop on the nearest bed and sleep and sleep…"

"Sleep," scoffed Mother Hopper. "I've scarcely slept myself since that Great Light appeared—but who wants to sleep at a time like this? You can always sleep when there's nothing else to do."

"Mother—you must have inherited some of your energy from perpetual motion," said Ellen, sinking into a chair. "But that food *does* smell good. Give me a bite of something and let me just go to sleep for awhile with my clothes on. I'll be all right in a few hours...but right now I can't even talk..."

"When a woman can't talk—that's serious," said Mother Hopper, taking charge.

Within fifteen minutes a groggy Ellen had some warm food inside her and was inside a warm bed.

"Gee, Mom," she remembered saying, as her voice trailed off into nothingness.

"I'm sure glad to have you here. The Green Man, too...but you'll have to entertain him. I just can't keep my eyes open another..."

AN UNEASY world slept the sleep of exhaustion in the welcome absence of the Green Light on this second night of the presence of the Green Men on earth. Humans were still greatly alarmed over the new world government, which had been announced, but they were reassured, at least, that they were not to suffer immediate physical harm or death. What punishment might be in store for many of them would have to be endured since there appeared to be no way of escape. They could not even expect protection from their own governments, which, in itself, was terrifying.

"Numar and his Green Men must be mighty powerful if they can take over all governments on earth as easy as this," said one human, expressing the conviction of many. "Guess we'll just have to go along—and hope for the best."

Officials at the Washington Municipal Airport had roped off the area around the amazing interstellar air monster to protect over-curious individuals from edging within the fifty foot danger zone, which Numar had warned would result in a human's instant electrocution. How many Green Men were aboard this quarter mile long ship, no one knew. Crewmembers and others were seldom seen—only Numar, who came and went as he had occasion.

Similar reports of the mysterious aloofness of the Green Men, aside from their Leaders, came from all foreign countries. They did not seek to exploit themselves and, after their spectacular entry upon the scene of Earth, were seriously concentrating upon their announced mission of saving humanity from itself. Their airships, in which they lived, remained objects of immense interest and speculation, humans traveling hundreds of miles to see them at close range.

One great good had already been accomplished, the effects of which only now began to be apparent. Imminent fear of a war between the United States and Russia had been removed. The peoples of the world realized that this threat had been swallowed up by what had seemed, at the moment and still might prove to be, a worse threat. Did Numar and his Green Men horde turn out to be a malevolent power, then destruction or slavery would come upon the world, anyway.

At present, the finest minds in every nation were studiously examining the Constitution of the United States of the World, which their governments had elected to support. The New Plan of Living, provided for by this Constitution was, by any past standards, so far advanced and so "radical" that few authorities would venture a public statement. There was consternation, however, in financial circles and predictions of utter ruin.

"The only difference between this Plan and Atomic War," one banker let himself be quoted, "is that the latter destroys you more quickly. Outside of that, I see devastation, either way."

ELLEN awakened the next morning with the telephone ringing. Before she could answer it, she was startled at hearing a woman's voice say: "Hello...no, this isn't Ellen...this is her mother I... What am *I* doing here...? Who are *you,* young man?"

Ellen laughed and slid out of bed. What a sleep she had had. And the world was still here—and so was her mother. It wasn't a dream—it was real!

"Who is it, Mom?" she called.

"That's just what I'm trying to find out," said Grandma Hopper. "How many men do you know?"

"What time is it?" asked Ellen.

"What difference does that make, do different ones call you at different times?"

Ellen hurried into her little living room and reached for the receiver.

"I'll take the call. Ummm. Coffee all made and everything. You're wonderful."

"Brownell?" said Mrs. Hopper into the phone. "Oh, is that so? Well, aren't you nice." She placed her hand over the mouthpiece, holding the French phone away from Ellen. "He wants to meet me. How old is he?"

Ellen screamed. "Oh, Mom—cut it out! That's Andy Brownell—you know, State Department—I've written you about him."

Grandma Hopper nodded, winking. "What's that? Well, I guess you know now it's no fairy story. That's what I came here for—to renew my acquaintance with him. No, I haven't talked with Ellen she's been too tired... You *are*... Say, that's fine. Mister Numar's going to turn this old world upside down—and you can help him do it!"

Ellen took a grip on the phone. "Listen, Mom—Andy probably has something important to tell me. Give up. Surrender."

"Here's my daughter," announced Mother Hopper. "Don't stay long on the phone now—breakfast's ready."

"Yes, Andy," spoke Ellen, then eyed her mother, laughing. "Quite a character is right. What's that...? Ten this morning? Me... Oh, that's fine... No. Who else? Katherine Barker?

Oh, Andy! Well, you know—she and I don't get along... I'm sorry... Of course... Foreign Relations Building...? Okay, I'll be there."

Ellen hung up the receiver and sat moodily reflecting. Mother Hopper, in from the kitchen, surveyed her.

"Well, do you want to tell or don't you?"

"Mom," said Ellen, "I've just been handed the most exciting assignment of my life. I'm to be one of the secretaries for the Council of Sixteen, which is having its first meeting this morning."

"That's Mister Numar's doing," guessed Mother Hopper, happily. "He knew you were my daughter. I'll have to thank him..."

"No," said Ellen. "Mister Numar told Andy to choose two secretaries. The only trouble is—the other one he chose was his own secretary—and she and I don't hit it off."

Mother Hopper studied her daughter for a moment, then chuckled, wisely.

"Both after the same man, are you...? Come have a cup of coffee. I always like people better after I've had something on my stomach."

CHAPTER FOURTEEN

AT TEN minutes to ten, two women met in a Conference Room at the Foreign Relations Building. They carried their shorthand notebooks and pencils. Each eyed the other defiantly.

"Nice morning, isn't it?" said Ellen, beating Katherine to the punch.

"That depends," answered Andy Brownell's secretary. "But since Russia and the United States have called off their war—how about us?"

"After what you've done to me?" charged Ellen.

"*What* have I done?" challenged Katherine.

"Well, I can't prove it, of course," retorted Ellen. "But I think that story in Dan Darrow's column..."

"We've only got ten minutes and the men will be in here," evaded Katherine. "Mr. Brownell thought we should sit at this separate little table and divide up the work any way we think best."

"Write your own ticket," said Ellen, dropping her equipment on the table.

The conference room had been prepared for the meeting. It had a main floor seating three hundred and a balcony, which could accommodate two hundred. The conference table was on a raised platform in the front of the room, with chairs set for seventeen places—eight on a side and the head chair reserved for Numar, who was to preside. Before each Council member's place was a microphone, connecting with the radio networks. The sessions, as Numar had stated, were to be open to the public and broadcast for all to hear. Even now a large crowd waited outside for admittance and hundreds would have to be turned away since all seats on the main floor had been reserved for notables from the sixteen nations directly concerned. But the whole world could follow every word of the proceedings by radio and television.

Special provision had been made for the Press with rows of tables on each side of the Conference table. But press coverage was limited to only top newspapermen and women, representing the different syndicates and associations. Numar did not wish to make a hippodrome of these world-changing sessions, just to please the merely curious since no meeting place could begin to accommodate the humans who desired to look on. The absence of any "behind-the-scenes" atmosphere, however, was apparent.

Massed at the front of the room, behind the seat, which Numar was to take, were the colorful flags of all nations. To the thoughtful observer these flags symbolized untold years of strife and turmoil as the humans, under them, had fought for what they thought to be right in little or big wars of aggression or defense—an historic record from which few nations, in all time, had long been exempt. When these flags were proudly carried in parade or on national holidays reference was often made to those "honored dead" who had given their lives that this nation might survive. Testimony again of Man's ages-old inhumanity to man.

BUT today there was commencing to be a new upsurge of hope. Perhaps this power greater than human would work where everything else, in all life history, had failed. Many had worshipped, in fear more than in love, and prayed to the various Gods of his superstition, imagination and evolving concept, picturing in his despair and desperate human need, deliverance from physical, mental and spiritual ills. But, always, in Man's blind, earnest gropings, it had taken something higher than himself to lift him from the morass of his own making. In this manner, humans had reached up from their wilderness toward a God in the heavens—a release from the miseries of Earth—and had followed, with great waves of religious fervor, the different enlightened souls who spoke of communion with God—such spiritual leaders as Zoroaster, Confucius, Buddha, Mohammed and Christ. Today, as in the past, Man was still seeking, for happiness had eluded him, security was not to be found, and all religious thought had not brought greater humanity of man for man. Something still must be lacking between Man and his relations with the one true God.

Perhaps this Super Being—Numar—knew the answer. Perhaps it might be contained in his New Plan of Living. Millions, with this newborn hope in mind, who had lost faith and trust in earth's rulers, prepared to listen to the first broadcast of Numar's Council of Sixteen. They would decide then how much faith to place in their new possible Savior.

At exactly ten o'clock the doors of the Conference Room in the Foreign Relations Building were opened and reporters and special guests took their seats. All remaining space was immediately made available, so long as it lasted, for the general public and these seats were gone in a flash. Thousands remained outside to hear the Council session via loudspeakers.

Special event radio announcers described the electrifying scene as the sixteen representatives of the different nations comprising the Council, walked to their places at the Conference table—young, competent appearing men of different races and colors.

As they stood beside their seats, the audience arose to join them when Numar, in his flowing white robe and tight-fitting turban was sighted striding quietly but majestically down the aisle. He smiled and bowed, to left and right, his green countenance radiating a feeling of great friendliness. All burst into applause.

While all were still standing, Numar lifted his hands and bowed his head.

"Oh, God—Father of All Creation," he addressed. "The one Great God of this Glorious, Unending Universe—be with Your creature, Man—on this planet, Earth—as he lifts his thoughts above fear and hate and greed and offers the true hand of Brotherhood to his fellow man, everywhere.

"Help Man to sense Your Power and Presence in his life as he opens the doors of his spirit to You—doors he has kept closed for centuries through Ignorance, Superstition and other forms of Wrong Thinking.

"Let Man realize that You *are* a Personal God, mindful of Man's ways, his down-fallings and uprisings—but that You can only come to Man as he comes to You, for Your Gift of Free Will has made Man a Free Agent to unite his Will with Your Will—or not, as he so chooses.

"Be with these Sixteen young men in their deliberations upon which the future hope of World Peace, Security and Happiness so largely depends.

"Let all Mankind come to appreciate that, when all hearts and minds have been tuned in on Your God-Power—free of fear and hate and prejudice—and filled with Love for Others as well as for You, their Creator—that there will then exist a Heaven on Earth as was intended from the Beginning.

"And, Dear Father of All, may I pray Your Guidance upon your humble and devoted servant—I, Numar, of the Planet Talamaya—as I enter upon this Sacred Mission. Amen."

NUMAR remained silent for a moment, then lifted his head and lowered his hands. Thus did he acknowledge allegiance to a power vastly greater than himself, to make it clear, at the outset that he, Numar, was not to be worshipped or regarded as a God. Those assembled in the Council Room and millions throughout the world, hearing Numar's words translated to their tongue by his Leaders, were strangely moved.

With all seated, this Man from Another Planet still stood and directed, quietly; "We will now have a calling of the roll. As I speak the name of the country or continent you represent, will you please rise and state your own name, in reporting your presence." Numar turned, smilingly, and nodded to his left, where representatives were seated in alphabetical order as their nations were listed.

"*Africa…*"

A dark-haired, dark-eyed young man, of military bearing arose.

"I, Melville Durban, am here."

He was greeted with applause as he bowed and was seated.

"*Asia…*"

The procedure was repeated, this time by a thin-faced darker complexioned individual.

"I, Riza Hakimi, am here."

"*Australia…*"

"I, Kenneth Warren, am here."

"*Canada…*"

"I, Jesse MacClintock, am here."

"*China…*"

"I, Foo Yung, am here."

"*Egypt…*"

"I, Hamid Bey, am here."

"*England…*"

"I, Everett Winston, am here."

"France..."

"I, Pierre DeVillers, am here."

"Germany..."

"I, Rudolph Frank, am here."

"Italy..."

"I, Anthony Giovanni, am here."

"India..."

"I, Nirmal Das, am here."

"Japan..."

"I, Yamishito Moto, am here."

"Netherlands..."

"I, Henrick Van Nostrand, am here."

"Russia..."

"I, Petrov Gouchevisky, am here."

"South America...."

"I, Ramon Lopez, am here."

"United States..."

"I, Andrew Brownell, am here."

EACH representative had risen, with quiet solemnity, answering to his country's call. There was something in this simple, straightforward procedure, which thrilled all who heard or saw it. Newsreel cameras were recording this most unusual event, as every action was also televised.

The initial formalities over, Numar now opened the session.

"I greet you Sixteen young men," he said. "As your Director and Advisor in the New Plan of Living, which is to be established on this earth.

"You may have wondered why you, individually, have been selected—and how your choice was arrived at. May I simply state, without endeavoring to explain something quite beyond your comprehension, that it is possible for me, with my developed powers, to make contact with your minds and to determine, therein, your potentialities."

The representatives glanced at one another in frank amazement, as the visible audience gasped.

"No Power is permitted to trespass upon Man's Free Will—so I cannot compel you to live up to the possibilities I see in each one of you. But, if you so choose to do, you can render undreamed of service to your fellow humans in your free and unselfish and unprejudiced association together.

"You have been chosen also because you each speak one language in common—English. Within the next few years every human must speak English as the Universal Language so that Man's understanding may not be cluttered up by false interpretations and vague meanings, which breed suspicion and distrust.

"Throughout the world, all local Councils must consist of young men, like yourselves, who can converse in English. This may in some instances, provide a temporary hardship inasmuch as some otherwise brilliant candidates might be chosen. As soon as they master English, they may qualify. However, at the moment, young men of equal integrity, though lesser intelligence or experience, may serve their country and the world more effectively, simply because of their ability to communicate with fellow members in *one tongue*.

"The primary importance of all peoples of the world speaking *one* language has been largely neglected or overlooked. It is *essential* to world understanding and cooperation."

Numar paused for a moment as all sixteen Council members sat, their attention fixed on him.

"When life becomes as involved and confused as it is at present, on this planet," Numar continued, "the only way human creatures may untangle their affairs is to proceed in the manner I am about to outline.

"Big United Nations organizations are too large and unwieldly—too motivated by special interests, too bound by age-old prejudices to function harmoniously. Observe the years of wrangling, which have ensued since the Second World War. Has any nation sacrificed anything voluntarily or changed its life or influence for the good of the whole? No—it has sought to preserve its holdings and its individual ways of living at all costs.

"I wish to make this point outstandingly clear. Will all newspaper and magazine correspondents please copy what I am about to say and put my words in your publications in capital letters?" Numar turned to the men and women at the press tables. They stiffened with expectation.

"All things which need correction on this earth must be changed together by all nations and all peoples at the same time.

"It is futile to attempt to correct one evil or wrong practice in one country or locality when the same or worse exists elsewhere.

"Passage of new laws to cope with crime does not cure the criminals. Methods and means must be introduced to remove from society the causes of crime—lack of education, poverty, bad environment, inequality of class and opportunity, poor home influence, improper spiritual training—and many other contributing factors.

"If only a few of these causes of crime are changed or removed, crime will continue unabated on this earth.

"But crime has become a part of big business today. It often is more politely called a racket and, in many countries is legalized in the form of betting and racing and various forms of gambling, which always enriches the few at the near ruination of the many.

"Crime enters government life at all levels, buying special privilege, votes, position, power, freedom from prosecution and intimidating or coercing great masses of a population.

"Such conditions cannot be changed unless the system and practices themselves are completely changed—not a little change here and a little change there—but one big change, including all necessary changes, everywhere—now!

"If you vaccinate to eliminate an epidemic, do you stop it by exempting those specially favored? If you do, the epidemic turns up again, possibly in a new form, and eventually rages as unchecked as ever.

"No, to build a new civilization of humans, freed forever from the evils of its past, you must lay an entirely new foundation.

"You have no other choice. The operation must be drastic, fundamental and immediate because all the ills of your world have become too concentrated in the body of humanity to be eliminated any other way.

"Unless you take these steps I am about to propose, in giving support to the constitution of the United States of the World, which your governments have sworn to uphold, nothing can stay the destruction of your planet.

"The third world war, so narrowly averted and only postponed by my arrival here with this new plan of living—will have brought an end to your civilization. Only an insane or uninformed human can deny it.

"Therefore, let me emphasize again that all necessary changes must be made simultaneously in all parts of this world. It cannot exist half slave and half free, half enlightened and half unenlightened, half and more starved and poverty-stricken. There is an abundance of the good things of life, rightly organized and distributed, which—free of commercial shackles and the influence of selfish interests—can properly care for all humans everywhere.

"Let us proceed then to set up this new plan of living so that man may be a friend to man on earth and God, the Father of us all, may add his blessings through our acts of brotherhood."

THE profound and far-reaching implications of Numar's statement left the sixteen Council Members speechless and the audience in the Conference Room likewise. The world outside was just as momentarily stunned at the suggested magnitude of the undertaking called for by Numar's announced New Plan of Living.

As if divining the great question rising up in the minds of millions, the Man from Another Planet, after a well-timed pause, said: "It will be far easier to accomplish *all changes* at once, than to attempt to establish them on a piece-meal basis. This is because all resistance to *change* is removed at the start. If you only clean half of a cesspool, the pool itself is still contaminated and, in a short time, becomes as unclean as it was before the operation. But if you clean up all conditions contributing to the filth of this cesspool, it remains clean and pure thereafter— providing the basic causes of these conditions have been eliminated.

"Removal of a grafting politician from office does not remove the conditions of graft surrounding that office, which may equally infect the next officer-holder. This New Plan of Living is designed to protect humans against their own weaknesses. If it is impossible to change human nature it is certainly possible to change the soil and environment in which humans are bred. This, in itself, will raise the quality of the human product over night.

"How can a Man, governed by the Merit System, steal from his fellow man? Merit is not transferable, it must be earned through honest effort. What a Man possesses, he is rightfully entitled to. It, therefore, cannot be taken away. The Man who refuses to work, automatically penalizes himself. Humans must strive to be worthy even of subsistence, if they are in good health, and the higher rewards of Merit are there for those who wish to put forth greater and greater effort."

Numar once more waited until he was sure his listeners, seen and unseen, had fully comprehended and reflected upon his declarations. Then he said:

"I have called this first session of the Council of Sixteen that you gentlemen, representing your respective countries and continents might get more fully acquainted with one another and the procedure expected of you.

"Because of the urgency of world conditions, this is not to be a diplomatic debating society. You young men of clear vision will be required to think and to act and to see to it that the provisions of this Constitution are executed by your governments and the governments of all other nations, as introduced.

"I desire that you pass a resolution requiring that the supplementary Council of All Other Nations be immediately set up to work with you. Members of this Council may be selected by their individual governments, just so they are under the age of thirty-five, as you are, and speak the English language.

"You gentlemen actually have control and direction of all International Affairs. You are not answerable to your individual governments—you are answerable to all humanity, for its destiny is in your hands.

"Your governments are under compulsion to carry out all recommendations you make and to see to it that their peoples likewise faithfully execute orders as given.

"I, Numar, represent the Power behind this Council in support of your commandments. Your governments and the peoples of the world must obey."

Numar paused, dramatically. "It is unfortunate that the threat of force must still be exercised but, in this case, it is for a most constructive purpose. No one will be hurt by the Power I am in position to call upon, except the despoilers of the human race. Their day, with establishment of this New Plan of Living on earth, is done!"

NUMAR, having completed his opening statement and remarks, seated himself. Ellen and Katherine, between them, had transcribed his entire talk.

The Russian member of the Council jumped to his feet, eyes flashing.

"Mister Numar!"

"Yes, Mr. Gouchevisky," recognized the Chairman from Another Planet.

"I know that the world is awaiting Russia's reaction to this Plan," he said. "I realize, too, we must all submit, whether we approve or not. But I wish to state, publicly, that I *do* approve.

Your Plan goes far beyond any plan of world government of which Russia has ever dreamed. I frankly don't know how to classify it...unless one might term it 'The Human Incentive System...' But I agree, if this Plan is to succeed, it must be put into full operation and maintained until the habits and customs and practices of Mankind can be re-educated. This means sacrifices and adjustments for all countries and all humans—but the goal is worth it. I, as a Russian, compulsion or no compulsion, subscribe whole-heartedly to this tremendous human engineering project and will be happy to co-operate with my fellow members in its establishment."

Petrov Gouchevisky sat down amid sudden, warm applause. It was a parade after that, with one after another of the Council Members paying tribute, Andrew Brownell, concluding with: "I am gratified at this one hundred percent show of genuine enthusiasm. It far exceeds the hopes of support I had. But, knowing human nature and human forces as I do, I am well aware that a mighty struggle lies ahead, even with Mr. Numar's wise counsel and direction. For Russia and the United States to at last be in agreement, even in Council Meeting, is a noteworthy achievement and a good omen for the future."

This brought appreciative laughter and more applause—then a burst of cheers when Brownell and Gouchevisky, by common impulse, though Ramon Lopez of South America sat between them, reached across in front of him—and *shook hands!*

This scene, carried to the peoples of the world by television and described by radio announcers, was wildly acclaimed.

Then Numar, calling the business part of the session to order, turned the chair over to the Council Member representing the first nation in alphabetical order—Melville Durban, of Africa.

"You gentlemen are familiar with the Constitution," was Numar's parting word. "You know the preparations, which must be made to put its provisions into effect. I will remain for consultation but it is your duty from now on to pass the resolutions and issue the orders, which within the period of a year, must place this entire Plan of Living in operation."

As Numar changed seats with Melville Durban, he was paid standing tribute by Council Members and all in the crowded Conference Room.

"Isn't this terrific?" said Ellen, moved.

"It's all show," said Katherine, guardedly. "Just a lot of lip service. They don't mean this—and you know it."

Ellen glanced at Petrov and Andy—studying the expressions on their faces.

"You think so?" she said. "Wanna bet?"

CHAPTER FIFTEEN

ONE of the spectators specially invited to this first session of the Council was a little old lady from California.

Ellen had left her mother outside in the corridor until Andy arrived, when her introduction to him brought immediate admittance for a seat in the balcony just before the crowd rushed in.

She sat, during the long conference, her attention focused on Numar, managing to whisper to those nearby that she "knew him personally...had known him for years." This statement caused many within hearing to make pinwheel motions with the index finger pointed toward their own heads, but Grandma Hopper didn't mind. She'd been laughed at before—*by experts!*

Nothing mattered to her but the glorious fact that she was seeing sensational earth history being made—these sixteen young men, under Numar's direction setting out to re-make the world.

And, at the conclusion, a moist-eyed old lady of a past generation waited at the door of the Conference room until everyone had been ushered out, for Numar to come down the aisle.

"Move on, Mother," said a guard in a kindly tone. "Mister Numar's not giving out any autographs."

"Who wants them," scoffed Mrs. Hopper. "I knew Mister Numar before you were born, young man. What's more, he said he wanted to see me."

"Yes, and I've really seen Santa Claus," said the guard, giving her a gentle push toward the door. "I mean the real one. Now, get going, little lady, we're not allowed..."

"Stop shoving," warned Grandma Hopper. "Or I'll have Mister Numar fire you."

The guard let out a burst of laughter. "Hey, Joe," he called to an associate. "Did you hear that? She's going to have the Green Man give me the bounce." The two men chuckled their amusement.

As they did so, a little after-conference of the Council broke up and Numar emerged, advancing down the aisle with cameramen pursuing him.

"Just a moment, please," called the photographers.

Numar was smiling. "I'm sorry, gentlemen...haven't you already found out? You're wasting your film on me."

Mrs. Hopper, dodging under the guard's arm, ran toward Numar and the photographers.

"It's no use, boys," she cried. "He won't photograph. Nobody could get his picture when he was here before! That's one reason people today wouldn't believe he was here. They think what I've been telling them was all a big hoax. But there stands the Green Man to prove I was telling the truth!"

"Mrs. Hopper," recognized Numar, striding toward her and extending his hand.

"Ye gods, Joe—she really does know him," exclaimed the guard.

"Well, Mister Numar,", said Grandma Hopper, appraising him. "You haven't changed a bit."

"Your *spirit* hasn't changed, either," said Numar. "But time has brought changes, as it always does with life on this planet."

"I've lived for this day," said Betty Annabelle Hopper. "Told my grandchildren about you and the amazing experience I had just as you said I'd do..." Then, with a twinkle in her eye.

"Not that it makes any difference, but do you still give out the same shock when you kiss that I received one time?"

NUMAR almost laughed aloud. "I presume I would if I did not think to insulate myself. Did you wish...?"

"No, thanks...but you might kiss my daughter just so she could know how it felt when I..."

"Mother!" protested Ellen, who was coming up the aisle.

"I'm sorry," smiled Numar. "I'm here this time on a serious mission. There is no time for entertainment or demonstrations."

"I didn't really mean it," laughed Mrs. Hopper. "Just wanted to give Ellen a scare. She didn't really believe... I'm certainly glad you came back, Mister Numar...you saved my reputation!"

"You were a great help to me, my last trip to earth," said Numar. "I shall never forget it."

"Say, it was all great fun," declared Mrs. Hopper. "Wish I had it all to live over again." Then, persuasively, "Mr. Numar—I know you're awfully busy—but won't you come up to Ellen's apartment while you're here—so we can visit and talk about 'old times?' I'm the only one left who remembers you—"

"I'm not accepting invitations but I *will* make an exception in your case," said Numar. "If you will give me your address and phone number, I will let you know when I can call."

"Ellen," ordered Mother Hopper. "Give it to him, quick!"

Ellen wrote the information on a piece of notepaper and handed it to the Green Man.

"Thank you," he said, and bowed. "I must be returning to my space ship now. I always communicate with my planet Talamaya about this time."

"You do?" Ellen exclaimed, astounded. "By radio?"

"By a higher form of it," smiled Numar. "It is possible for me to elevate my consciousness so that I can annihilate time and space. Humans won't reach this evolution for some millions of years yet—but this faculty is even now, lying dormant in your minds, awaiting future development."

All within earshot gasped their amazement.

"You will be hearing from me one of these days," Numar promised, and then, shaking hands once more with Mrs. Hopper, he said: "What do *you* think of the New Plan of Living?"

"*I* think," said Mother Hopper, staunchly, loud enough for all to hear, "that anything you're behind is all right."

Newspapers throughout the world were filled with reports of the first meeting of earth representatives with the Man From Another Planet. Headlines and stories were read or explained to all humans, who could talk or think of nothing else.

WORLD CHANGES MAPPED BY COUNCIL OF SIXTEEN
ORDERS ISSUED TO RULERS TO PUT PLAN IN EFFECT

First steps were taken by the Council of Sixteen, acting under the Constitution of the United States of the World, to put the New Plan of Living into operation.

Orders were issued the governments of all nations to organize and conduct an inventory of citizens of every age for the purpose of determining their conditions of health, individual ability, education, economic circumstances and housing facilities.

This inventory is to be in preparation for introduction of a worldwide Merit System, which eventually will replace the present methods of currency exchange.

Drastic changes are also to be instituted in systems of world education—committees of prominent laymen and educators of every country being required to revise all present methods of study and teaching so that the equivalent of a High School education may be secured by each boy or girl by the age of fifteen.

Provision is to be made at once for the teaching of English, as the universal language, in every country on earth and even in the remote corners and by-ways of the planet.

THE GREEN MAN RETURNS

All laws, civil and criminal are to be overhauled and so revamped, eliminated or consolidated as to standardize their regulation of all humans in all nations. There will be one set of Divorce, Traffic and Crime laws, for example, applicable to each individual nation.

WORLD COMMODITY MARKET
TO BE ESTABLISHED

To bring about a balance of Necessary Foods and Articles—an International Pool or Surplus Commodity Market is to be set up wherein all needy nations may purchase or trade in other commodities or resources in exchange for those such countries lack.

Universal values are to be placed upon Foods and Articles and world control exercised over the raising of crops and livestock so that the Laws of Supply and Demand can be equalized insofar as it is humanly possible—and speculation and exploitation reduced to a minimum.

NEWS stories went on to describe change after change which would alter, in time, the entire thought, practice and economy of humans everywhere.

Editorials, however, since Numar, the world's new self-appointed ruler, had placed no restriction upon freedom of speech or expression—cast grave doubts about the whole program. It was universally admitted that the peoples of the world could offer no resistance to this Plan, which was being imposed, yet a calamity of gigantic proportions was being predicted.

In the face of these gloomy comments, Numar's Leaders in all nations calmly proceeded to complete organization of the local Councils and to see to it that orders from the Council of Sixteen in Washington were carried out by such government or private agencies as were concerned.

At the end of the "unofficial three day holiday" period announced by Numar, upon his arrival, the marts of the world re-opened for business and the stock market in New York immediately indulged in a wild break of panic-stricken selling.

If the Profit System was to be eliminated, and money itself to be destroyed, then what Man possessed in the way of property—real estate, a business, a manufacturing plant, anything tangible, which could assure productivity, might still have value. Many, gambling that no force, cosmic or man-made, could do away with the money system—liquidated their holdings in business and industry, fearing seizure or government operation and placed their trust in the thousands or millions of accumulated cash on hand. Any human's guess was as good as the next one's since no precedent existed for the present situation on earth.

The repercussion on world trade was evident almost immediately. More buying came to an abrupt stop. Why buy merchandise when there was no guarantee that the markets would continue to exist, over night? Why pay out any more money, which might not come back? Fear began to choke the commercial arteries and slow down every human activity to the point of paralysis.

The money powers of the world were striking in revolt against this New Plan of Living. Let Numar and his fellow Green Men cope with this, if they could.

A week, then two weeks passed—during which world tension grew. There were widespread threats of disorder, unemployment, want and panic.

Suddenly all radio networks were again cut off and the Voice of Numar mysteriously spoke out of the atmosphere:

"Greetings—all people of Earth!

"You are to keep working, as before, until this New Change is put into effect. If you do, you will suffer no individual hardship; if you do not, the inconvenience and privation you experience will be of your own making.

"No changes will be introduced until all basic changes are ready to operate in unison.

"I will announce the date of the Great Change so that you may prepare for it.

"You have been reading and hearing many warnings of world calamity. What do you think you people were approaching under your present system—a heaven or a hell upon earth?

"May I remind you once more that the Third World War would now be raging were it not for my presence here?

"No human powers are capable of criticizing this New Plan of Living or making dire prophesies about it—since this Plan has never been tried.

"Your ancestors predicted that boats made of iron and steel would never replace wooden boats because they would sink. They predicted that nothing heavier than air could ever fly. Limited by lack of vision, imagination, actual knowledge and experience—they could not foresee many of the wonders you now accept as common place.

"Do not fear the hysterical prophesies of those who cry out against Change today. They see only the possibility of a personal loss to them—not a gain for All Humanity, including themselves.

"Be patient while all preparations for your Liberation from old-age conditions are being completed. I promise you, in a short while, as you reckon time on earth, Greater Happiness and Security and Peace than you have ever known.

"I, Numar, Your Liberator, have spoken!"

THE quiet but powerful assurance of this message had a calming effect upon millions. It served notice upon selfish world interests that Numar was undeterred in his determination to put through the New Plan of Living, regardless of such obstacles in the way of a "slow-down" up to actual worldwide revolt, as might be engineered against him.

Desperate, a committee of three prominent men, representing Banking, Industrial and Business interests, called at the office of Andrew Brownell in the State Department.

"I suppose you know, if this sort of thing keeps up much longer, you won't have any country," said Banker Kendall. "Haven't you any backbone at all? Why don't you speak out against this system, Numar or no Numar. Even a child can see it's going to ruin anything of any value anywhere!."

"But what you gentlemen can't see," defended the State Department's bright young man, "is that the present world values are going to be replaced with a *higher set of values.*"

"Bunk of the worst kind," denounced Industrialist Simpson. "We're sure of the values we've got. We've taken years to build them up. We've got millions invested—billions!"

"For which you'll be given credit according to the new standards," said Andy. "We're working on an Appraisal Plan, which will be a measuring stick for determining the credit to be allowed all business, industrial, agricultural, professional, trade and labor activities in all countries. The credit rating will be set up in direct accordance with the standards of living now existing or, at present, possible in each nation."

The three prominent committee members exchanged disturbed glances.

"The more we hear of this, the more impossible it gets," said the representative of Big Business, Mr. Sparks. "I had always considered you one of our sanest, straightest thinking young diplomats, Mr. Brownell. I can't understand your complete backward somersault. What's happened? Has this man from another planet hypnotized you—or scared you to death?"

Andy smiled, wearily. "He has given me a new perspective," was his reply. "The ability to think, free of any world influence or prejudice. If you gentlemen once could catch this vision you wouldn't be afraid of what you were going to *lose*—you would be enthused over what you were going to *gain.*"

Banker Kendall stood up. "We're wasting our time here," he said bluntly. "We might as well have embraced Communism and been done with it."

"The Communists have laid no claims to this Plan," said Andy. "There is too much work attached to it, too much honest effort involved, too great an opportunity for freedom of thought and expression and advancement. This Plan is not vindictive. It is against no honest class or interests. It is for the good of all, through the cooperation of all."

"Come on, gentlemen," said Industrialist Simpson. "Let's be getting out of here."

THE three committee members turned on their heels and stalked out of Andrew Brownell's office. They stopped, in the outer room, however, to have words with his secretary.

"Miss Barker," addressed Big Businessman Sparks, "how much influence do you have with Mr. Brownell?"

"That depends," said Katherine.

"If it's a fair question, do you approve of what is going on?"

"Well," hesitated Katherine, "in a way, I do—in a way, I don't. I'm frankly quite bewildered, at this point."

"I should think you would be," said Banker Kendall. "And apparently Mr. Brownell is more than bewildered—he's been *mesmerized!* All sixteen of that Council must have come under Mister Numar's influence. That's the only way to account for their complete submission."

"But what can they do against such a power?" asked Katherine.

"We'd do something if we were in their place," said Industrialist Simpson.

"Just what—for instance?" asked Katherine.

"Well—we'd try to reason with Mister Numar first," volunteered Big Businessman Sparks, after each of the trio had waited for someone else to speak. "Get him to modify this Plan—explain to him that not being a human, himself, he can't realize it's just not possible to make such changes. We believe he's too intelligent and too fair-minded not to listen…"

The secretary of Andrew Brownell shook her head.

"I'm afraid, gentlemen, that this wouldn't work. Mister Numar knows so much more than we do, our arguments wouldn't stand up."

Banker Kendall leaned across the desk and lowered his voice. "Miss Barker—your boss, Mr. Brownell, has an opportunity to go down in history as the world's greatest hero. This Numar must, somehow, be outwitted. If dissension should break out among the Council of Sixteen, this might delay and upset matters. In that time we may be able to work out a method of defense and if Mr. Brownell can be brought out from under Mister Numar's spell—he could lead the opposition. You are in a key position to be extremely helpful. Can we count on you to keep your eyes and ears open and do all you can to aid us, as the opportunities arise?"

Katherine hesitated. She was confronted by three of the country's biggest men. If they were right—and if Andy and fellow Council members no longer had any judgment of their own...

"You may as well know," confided Big Businessman Sparks, "we are in touch with powerful interests abroad—and they are working on members of the Councils being formed in their countries. We'll soon have a resistance group set up to operate under cover until we are ready to make a fight for it. God only knows what Numar and his Green Men will do to us, once we are stripped of all power and possession."

This, of course, could be possible. Mister Numar was charming, spell-binding, in fact. Especially friendly to Ellen, because of her mother—that impossible Mrs. Hopper!

"All right, gentlemen," Katherine heard herself saying, guardedly. "I—I'll do what I can."

"Good," said Banker Kendall. "We'll keep in touch. If our way of life is to be saved—or any semblance of freedom on this entire planet—it must be done before this Plan goes into effect."

"Good day, Miss Barker," said Industrialist Simpson. "I'm glad there are a *few* Americans who can't be hypnotized or intimidated."

"Numar's threat to destroy our planet is being taken too seriously," said Big Businessman Sparks. "He put on a great astronomic display, that's true—but this old earth has existed through millions of years and it's my opinion that we've been terrorized into submission by a crafty enemy who is using this Plan he's introducing to make us all subjects to *his* will."

"It could be," conceded Katherine. "And I can assure you that if Andy—I mean, Mr. Brownell—ever comes to this conclusion, he'll join forces with you to overthrow Numar and his horde, if it can be done."

"That's fine," said Banker Kendall. "Let's go, gentlemen— we have a tremendous lot to do—and not so much time to do it in."

CHAPTER SIXTEEN

THE woman who successfully predicted the appearance of the Great Light and the return to earth of the Green Man, had to wait weeks before Numar's promised visit to her daughter Ellen's Washington apartment materialized.

Tremendous things were happening in the world. Grandma Hopper observed them all with growing interest and concern. There was more and more evidence of possible rebellion as humans, everywhere, were put under pressure by their governments with preparations going forward, on a colossal scale, for launching of the New Plan of Living.

"Poor Mister Numar," said Mrs. Hopper, more than once. "I'd hate to be in his kind of work—if he jumps from planet to planet, like some great efficiency expert, and tries to straighten things out as he's doing here. I can begin to understand how God must feel when He creates an earth, with creatures on it like us—possessing wonderful possibilities for development— and then we don't make use of them. I imagine He must almost be tempted, at times, to destroy it all and start all over again. But the fact that He doesn't must mean that He loves us, just the same and wants to give us every chance. I don't think I'd have that much patience."

It lacked but a week of three months to the day of his arrival when Numar made his all-important announcement to the peoples of the world.

"One week from today," he told the world with his Leaders in all nations translating the message for him, "the day of the Great Change will be here. It is to be an international holiday and is always to be celebrated on this Earth hereafter as "Liberation Day."

"You are to gather in your public parks or such public places as designated by your local authorities, to witness the burning of all paper money. Gold and silver coins and other metals used for currency are to be melted up and used for other purposes.

"Beginning tomorrow your Merit Cards will be distributed to you and banks and government agencies, in whatever zone you live, will hold your already established credits on deposit.

"You will thus surrender your money, which will have no purchasing power a week from today—and possess instead, your own individual valuation based upon your rating in the community.

"On Liberation Day, a percentage of you who are over forty will be retired from your trade or physical labor and can then live on your Guaranteed Subsistence plus such Merit Rating as you have earned through your years of employment. Within a year, all over forty will have been retired and, after that time, men and women who have devoted their lives in the trades and at unskilled labor will automatically be retired upon reaching that age.

"Every opportunity is being provided for those of you over forty to continue to lead useful lives in taking advantages of new opportunities to learn; to teach; to enjoy rest, relaxation, recreation, entertainment; to travel; to serve your community, your nation and the world.

"Your retirement, after having given twenty-five of the most vigorous years of your life in work and helping produce and bring up the New Generation, enables your places to be taken by younger citizens who heretofore have not found sufficient opportunities awaiting them in their earlier years to permit them to assume responsibilities for which they have long been qualified.

"Those of older years will no longer be dependent upon their young for support or shelter. This will free much of the unhappiness and inequity of family relations and make it possible for each married couple to enjoy the privacy of their own home.

"Emphasis is to be placed upon prevention of physical and mental ills through proper medical attention, available to all, and hospitalization, as needed—so that, in time, institutions for the criminally insane, feeble-minded and physically afflicted persons will be reduced to the minimum.

"Do not expect miracles after the Great Change is put into operation. It will require time for it to function smoothly and for humans everywhere to adapt themselves to the new practices and duties and responsibilities.

"Remember, however, that this Plan of Living is your last chance for Peace and Happiness on this earth. Your liberation from the age-old ills of the past it at hand—if you are willing to work for it. If not, your human race will not long survive.

"Every attempt is now being made and will be made by certain earth forces to sabotage this Plan. Some of them are sincere in the belief that it can only result in complete and devastating failure.

"Can they point to a better plan, which is more certainly designed to eliminate most of the basic causes of crime, poverty, religious and racial prejudice, economic maladjustment and unhappiness on this earth?

"They are silent in the face of this challenge for your human society, as organized and developed today, compels the poor to oppose the rich and the rich to prey upon the poor. Such a society must always war against itself—destroying its set of false values and building them up again and again for new destruction.

"But, now, with the Merit System, each human being, for the first time, has a value of his own—not judged by possession or lack of money—and this value *cannot* be taken away.

"Do not fear. Instead, rejoice that your day of Liberation is so near—and that you can participate, at last, on a basis of equality with every fellow human on earth.

"I, Numar, your Liberator, have spoken!"

THE long awaited telephone call from the Green Man followed shortly upon conclusion of his world broadcast and caught Grandma Hopper completely by surprise.

"You mean...you could really come over to visit with us for a while this evening?" she repeated. "Oh, Mister Numar, that would be wonderful. Ellen isn't home yet for dinner but I know she'll be delighted...and there are so many questions I meant to ask you on your first trip here that I didn't get around to...well, if eight o'clock suits you, it's fine for us... All right...see you then."

Mother Hopper hung up the receiver and did a couple of dance steps in expression of her school girl excitement. Ellen was presented the news before she could get her apartment door completely open.

"Just think of it, Ellen—we're being honored with the only personal visit Numar's paying to humans on this planet. Too bad he doesn't eat. I'd like to bake him a good old American apple pie or a cake or something special."

"Well, he shouldn't be too hard to provide for—when he doesn't eat or drink or smoke," said Ellen, "but, good heavens, mother—what do you talk about to a Being tike that for an evening?"

"Talk," said Mrs. Hopper, "that's the least thing I worry about."

A sudden thought hit Ellen and her face lighted up.

"Oh, mother—it seems selfish to just be having this wonderful opportunity to visit with Mister Numar by ourselves.

I just know Petrov and Andy would give anything for a chance to see him this way. Do you suppose...?"

"Of course, dear. I'm sure Mister Numar wouldn't mind at all. Call them up and see if they can come."

Ellen flew to the phone. It was late afternoon but quite possibly the two men in question were still at their offices. Petrov was—and she was put through to him at once. Yes— he'd be delighted to meet Mr. Numar. She could expect him shortly after eight. Now to get Andy.

"Mr. Brownell is not here—but I'm expecting him back," said a woman's voice, Katherine's, of course. "Who's calling, please?"

"This is Ellen."

"Oh, yes...stupid of me...I should have recognized your voice. Anything important?"

"Yes. Mister Numar's dropping in this evening to visit Mother and me," announced Ellen, enjoying the opportunity to rub it in. "I thought this would be a good time for Mr. Gouchevisky and Andy to sit down and really get acquainted with him."

"Very interesting," said Katherine. "Have you invited Mr. Gouchevisky yet?"

"Yes, he's accepted," replied Ellen. "Will you tell Andy when he comes in? We'll be looking for him any time after eight."

"Right you are," said Katherine. "I'll get word to him."

PETROV arrived before the guest of honor. He was his usual handsome self and made an instant hit with Mother Hopper by presenting her with a box of flowers—American beauties—while to Ellen he gave a box of candy.

"I'm liking the Russians more and more," said Grandma Hopper.

Petrov smiled. "An accident of birth made me a Russian. It might have made you Russians, too, or Germans or Italians or Indians, Negroes—any race or color."

"But it *didn't*," said Mrs. Hopper. "So what does that prove?"

"It proves," said Petrov, seriously, "that we can't help being what we are—and that, therefore, we shouldn't hold it against any other human for being what he is. Now, thanks to Mister Numar, we are commencing to think in terms of our all being *humans*, with an equal right to the good things of life, instead of separated into these different races and colors and creeds and paired off against each other on the basis of religious and racial hatreds or political differences."

Ellen heard a sudden commotion in the street and ran to the window.

"Mister Numar's arriving," she announced. "He's in the special limousine the President turned over for his use—and he's attracting the usual crowd. No wonder he doesn't go many places."

"That's not at all like he was when he came to this earth before," said Grandma Hopper. "He made public appearances and was willing to let the whole world see him. But after he got everyone's attention and predicted the coming of the Great Light, he left this earth in a hurry."

Petrov nodded. "That was probably what he really came for, at that time. And he'll no doubt leave just as quickly when this job is done."

"When it's *done?*" repeated Ellen, dubiously. "Do you think, Peter—that'll be *ever?*"

Russia's member of the Council of Sixteen shook his head. "No, not by us. We'll always have to keep working at this Plan. But I think Mister Numar's just come here to give us the pattern of right living—and once he's introduced it, carrying it out will be up to us. That's a point I'd like to make clear tonight—if he'll talk about it."

Ellen's phone commenced an excited ringing. The desk clerk's voice: "Miss Hopper, Mister Numar is calling."

"Send him up, please," said Ellen, trying to remain matter-of-fact. Then, turning to Petrov, she said: "I've asked Andy here, too. You don't mind?"

THERE was just the slightest hesitation before Petrov's reply.

"Not at all. The United States and Russia are getting along on a very friendly basis since Mister Numar has taken over. I shall enjoy an evening in Mr. Brownell's company."

The doorbell rang and Mrs. Hopper was first on her feet.

"Let *me*," she commanded. "He's really coming on my invitation."

She opened the door as Ellen and Petrov stepped back—and there stood the Green Man, bowing and smiling.

"Mister Numar," exclaimed Grandma Hopper. "It's so nice to see you. Come in... Come in... You know Ellen...and Mr. Gouchy—something or other—Peter, my daughter calls him."

Numar, starting into the apartment, stopped, his dark eyes growing momentarily darker.

"Yes," he said. "I have met Mr. Gouchevisky and I have deep admiration for him, but I am sorry to say I cannot meet him here...or any other member of the Council. Affairs are in too sensitized a state on the eve of the Great Change. Such a meeting might be wrongly interpreted as evidence of favoritism on my part. This, you can now understand, is the reason why I, and my fellow Leaders, have avoided all social engagements and have remained free of contact with all humans, except for the official association necessary in the performance of our mission. I, therefore, regret that I must leave at once."

As Numar turned to go, Petrov spoke.

"It will not be necessary for you to depart," he volunteered. "I understand and respect your position perfectly, Mister Numar—and I shall be happy to remove myself, to save any possible embarrassment."

"That is kind of you," said Numar.

"I'm terribly sorry," apologized Ellen. "I didn't mean to do anything I shouldn't. I just knew Mr. Gouchevisky and Mr. Brownell would be so happy to share our visit with you…"

"I cannot remain if Mr. Brownell is to be here either," warned Numar.

"Well, I'll just have to tell him, when he calls, that he can't come up," decided Ellen.

Petrov was at the door, hat in hand.

"Good evening, Mister Numar," he said, bowing. "I am sure Miss Hopper was innocent of wishing to cause any complications when she invited Mr. Brownell and myself…"

Numar smiled. "I accept her apology, Mr. Gouchevisky. It would be a pleasure, were circumstances different, to visit with many humans on this earth. But this will have to remain for my next visit—if all goes well."

"I won't live until that one," said Grandma Hopper. "I can predict that, right now."

"Good night, Petrov," called Ellen, as he turned down the hall, toward the elevators. "I can't tell you how badly I feel…"

"Think nothing of it," he smiled. "Have a good time. Be seeing you."

BUT Ellen couldn't have a "good time" after this. She felt that Andy would be calling at any moment and she would have to head him off from coming up to the apartment. Even Grandma Hopper, usually a voluble talker, lost her spark and had little to say. Numar politely remained for about half an hour, then excused himself.

When he had gone, Ellen still had not heard from Andy, but she was tremendously relieved that he had not shown up.

"I can't understand, though, if he couldn't have made it, why he didn't phone me back," Ellen told her mother. "That's not like him."

"Oh, well, everybody's got so much on their minds today," said Mrs. Hopper, "there's no explaining anything. I'm so disappointed that our meeting with Mister Numar turned out to be such a fizzle. I never thought he'd object to your having your men friends in. Just to think—I looked forward to such a meeting all these years—and now it's over—what is there to show for it?"

"Mother, it's my fault for even suggesting calling Petrov and Andy," said Ellen. "This was your party, not mine, in the first place. I'll never forgive myself."

"Well, what's done is done," said Grandma Hopper, philosophically. "I can see Mister Numar's point...he's not going to do anything that has any chance of upsetting his world plan. After all, that means more to him and to us than a good visit."

Ellen finally heard from Andy, not that night but the following morning. His phone call got her out of bed.

"Have you seen the morning papers?" he demanded.

"Not yet," said Ellen, trying to get her eyes open.

"Then let me read you something," said Andy. "'Secret Conference Held Between Numar and Russian...'"

"Oh, no!" cried Ellen.

"Listen!" commanded Andy, and read further: "'Despite assurances to the press and public that no secret meetings could be held or secret diplomacy employed, Numar and Petrov Gouchevisky, Russian member of the Council of Sixteen, met at the apartment of Miss Ellen Hopper last night. The significance of this meeting is not known but much speculation has been touched off as a result. Miss Hopper will be remembered as the young woman who figured in a top Washington scandal some months ago when this same Mr. Gouchevisky was picked up for questioning by Military Intelligence, and Miss Hopper was found with him, in his apartment. While she was discharged from her position as a White House secretary, she reappeared on the scene with the arrival of the Green Men, being chosen as one of the secretaries for the newly formed Council of Sixteen, which Mr. Numar is directing. Miss Hopper's mother is no less a mysterious personage with her claim to having known Numar on his previous visit to this planet. Mother and daughter have been living together in Miss Hopper's apartment and they were apparently hostesses at this meeting. It is rumored that Numar especially desired to privately commend Mr. Gouchevisky on Russia's being the first great country to complete inventory of all her people, preparatory to introduction of the Merit System. However, this supposition has not been confirmed.'"

ELLEN, numb and sick at heart, heard the news account through.

"*Oh, Andy!*" she said, and caught back a sob.

"How did this meeting come about?" asked the United States member of the Council of Sixteen.

"Why, don't you know?" said Ellen. "I phoned your office—told Katherine you were invited, too."

"I never received the invitation," said Andy. "First I've heard of it."

"I can't understand that. Katherine said you were out and that she'd get word to you."

"She was gone when I returned—but there was no note on my desk."

Ellen put a hand to her head. She felt faint.

"Well, the way it turned out, it's a good thing you didn't know, I guess...it saved you from getting in a mess."

"Did Mister Numar want to see Mr. Gouchevisky and me?" Andy persisted.

"No—it was all my idea," confessed Ellen. "He was coming over to see mother—for old times' sake—and I got excited and thought how swell it would be for you and Petrov to sit in on the meeting, too. I phoned Petrov and he accepted and came...but when Numar arrived, he said, right away, he couldn't stay, with Petrov there..."

"And so?"

"So Petrov told Mister Numar that he would leave instead of him—and that's what he did—immediately!"

There was a throbbing pause on the wire.

"Well," said Andy, "the fat's in the fire now. There's been terrific tension and suspicion underneath, despite the fact that things have been making progress on the surface. Everyone has been watching for Numar to show some hint of favoritism—especially to the United States or Russia—and the opposition will jump on this little incident and make the most of it."

"Yes," conceded Ellen. "I can see that…but if I made a public explanation…"

"Haven't you done about enough now?" snapped Andy. "Ellen, what in the world could you have been thinking of?"

"I guess," said Ellen, dully, "I just wasn't thinking at all."

"Well, don't talk if the papers call and don't see any reporters. Leave matters as they are. I'll try to gloss this over as best I can."

Andy hung up and Ellen burst into tears.

About the same time another young woman was receiving a telephone call.

"Hello, Miss Barker, this is Mr. Kendall. Is your boss in yet?"

"No, Mr. Kendall, not yet."

"Good. That's a very exciting newsbreak in the papers this morning. Know anything about it?"

"I should say I do. Miss Hopper phoned last night, inviting Mr. Brownell to the same meeting. It didn't sound like quite the right thing to me—so I forgot to tell Mr. Brownell—and, of course, he didn't go."

"Fine business," commended Banker Kendall. "That little move on your part may have put us in exactly the position we want. Do you think Mr. Brownell would have gone—if you hadn't—well—stopped him?"

"He might have," admitted Katherine.

"This Miss Hopper appears to have quite a little influence…"

Another phone commenced ringing. "Excuse me, Mr. Kendall. I'm here alone and the other phone…hang on a second." She switched to the other line. "Hello… Oh, yes, Mr. Brownell."

Andy's voice came on the line. "Miss Barker, I've just talked with Miss Hopper. Did she phone last night inviting me…?"

"Oh, yes—she did. I—I'm dreadfully sorry, Andy—I had several things come up and it completely slipped my mind."

"That was a pretty unfortunate slip."

"Do you think so? I thought you might consider it pretty lucky, after what happened."

"Not at all—if I'd been there, along with Mr. Gouchevisky, the two biggest powers would have been represented, and *no one* has ever accused the United States and Russia of being in collusion. This whole incident might have been overlooked. Now it appears there is going to be hell to pay."

"I'm sorry," said Katherine. "I believe you'll find, when you get down to the office, that you've been placed in a very strong position. There's been a loss of confidence—but not in you— or our country, in fact, people seem to be looking to us—"

"JUST a minute," cut in Andy. "I've noticed, of late, a growing disposition on your part, Miss Barker, to try to do my thinking and deciding for me. This is something I won't tolerate. One more incident like this and you are no longer my secretary."

"Yes, Andy—I mean—Mr. Brownell!" she faltered. "I've only had your best interests in mind. I've always tried to protect you."

"I don't need or want protection!" blazed Andy. "I'm coming straight to the office. Good-bye!"

The receiver slammed in her ear. Considerably shaken, Katherine switched back to the waiting Banker Kendall.

"That was Mr. Brownell," she volunteered.

"That so? How does he feel about this happening?"

"Pretty upset, of course."

"Eyes opened to the underhanded tactics of Russia, eh?"

"No—and you mustn't interpret what happened that way," said Katherine, suddenly alarmed. "This wasn't any privately arranged meeting between Mr. Gouchevisky and Mr. Numar. Not when Mr. Brownell was supposed to be there, too."

"Well, the public will look at it that way and, of course, they really did meet," said Banker Kendall. "You did exactly right in preventing Mr. Brownell from attending. Great service. For your information, Miss Barker, we're pretty well organized now all over the world. This Liberation Day may not be such a picnic for Mister Numar. We have a Plan of our own, which may blow his Plan of Living right off this earth."

"I'd be interested to hear about it," said Katherine, her head pounding.

"Later, Miss Barker...later. Keep up the good work. You'll be hearing from us."

This telephone call completed, the second young woman that morning burst into tears.

At the session of the Council of Sixteen, with Foo Yung of China presiding, the expected fireworks exploded.

Rudolph Frank, German member, addressed the chair and asked to bring before the Council the newspaper reports of last night's secret meeting with Petrov Gouchevisky and the honorable Mister Numar, which allegedly took place in the apartment of one of the Council's secretaries, Miss Ellen Hopper.

Mr. Frank was supported in his request by Hamid Bey of Egypt, Everett Winston of England, Pierre DeVillers of France and Nirmal Das of India. A resolution was framed and passed, demanding an explanation of the incident.

Petrov Gouchevisky and Ellen Hopper testified, declaring the whole affair to have been highly and needlessly exaggerated and explaining just how the episode occurred. Both swore that Numar expressed his displeasure and embarrassment and that Mr. Gouchevisky immediately withdrew.

Andrew Brownell, then speaking for the United States, stated, emphatically: "This is a cheap attempt to arouse age-old feelings of distrust and suspicion among us and to upset our amicable relations at the eleventh hour when this New Plan of Living is about to be launched. I am positive, gentlemen that nothing transpired between Mr. Gouchevisky and Mister Numar—and that the whole matter was an innocent incident, as described. I, myself, would have been at this meeting had my secretary not forgotten to inform me of my invitation. My presence there should have removed all criticism but because Mr. Gouchevisky happened to have been the only member of this Council present, sinister motives are impugned.

"I wish to go on record as declaring that I have every confidence in Mr. Gouchevisky's integrity and also in the honor and complete impartiality of Mister Numar. As for Miss Ellen Hopper, she is the victim of her own enthusiastic admiration of Mister Numar and her desire that Mr. Gouchevisky and I, her friends, should share his visit. Beyond this there is nothing for the most rabid rabble-rouser to make capital of—and I trust that you gentlemen of the Council will speedily exonerate all concerned and grant them a vote of confidence."

ANDY seated himself amid applause and the vote of confidence was soon taken. Numar then rose to address the Council and another crowded chamber.

"It is to be expected, as we approach the climax of our efforts to inaugurate this New Era in human thinking and conduct, that increasing attempts will be made to create discord, disunity and distrust," he said. "An Old Order never dies gracefully and a New Order is never born without trial and suffering. Only because this New Plan of Living is worldwide can we hope for success. Otherwise the Old Order disguises itself, moves into parts of the world where resistance to the New Order or protection from it exists, and—in time—develops new strength to again sweep the planet.

"I give you my assurance now—as I have in repeated utterances since coming to your Earth—that no force or combination of forces can prevent this Plan of Living from being established. Once set up throughout the world, you humans placed in control will be charged with the responsibility of making it work.

"Your pledge of confidence here today should set an example to the peoples of the world who have been so easily panicked in the past by false rumors, which have played upon their deep-seated feelings of hate and prejudice.

"Once this Plan is in operation, such feelings will commence to vanish as each individual is judged, not as to his race or religion or color—but as to his own personal value—ability—character.

"Remember, gentlemen, your attitude here can upset the balance of the world in this critical period. If you do not remain self-assured, self-confident, self-disciplined and united in purpose, you cannot lead the peoples of all nations successfully through this Great Change.

"I congratulate you all upon your magnificent courage, steadfastness and harmonious co-operation, thus far demonstrated. May you meet the test on the day of Liberation!"

CHAPTER SEVENTEEN

REFUTATION of false charges or damaging news stories even when public apologies or denials are made, seldom remove from mass consciousness the suggestion of evil or misconduct, which the first publication has created.

This was true in the case of the Gouchevisky-Numar "secret meeting" story since strong feelings of animosity and distrust still existed in the minds of millions of Americans and Russians toward each other.

Once stirred up, these feelings were communicated to millions more, sympathizers and supporters of either the United States or Russia.

The old, old adage that "where there's smoke there has to be some fire," left many convinced that some strange move had been attempted by Russia to gain some advantage with Numar in the world changes about to be effected.

And so, a world already grim, uncertain and uneasy over the Great Change, which was to be visited upon all humans, whether desired or not, greeted the proclaimed "Day of Liberation" with almost hysterical misgivings.

Washington, D. C. was to be the starting point of similar ceremonies to be held throughout the world. Cities and communities, big and small, were to stage great bonfires of paper money to mark the end of the Currency Regime.

In Potomac Park, immense piles of paper money, brought from the government mints, were stacked skyward. The banks of the city had cleaned out their tills and vaults. Thousands of citizens marched by the mountains of money and tossed their own greenbacks upon the ever-growing mounds. Other thousands feverishly hid their money away, unable to believe that these pieces of paper would ever lose their value.

Each citizen now held his own Merit Credit Card and Merit Check Books containing different stamps of Merit Points, which he was to exchange for purchases according to their established point values. But, somehow, these stamps looked worthless in comparison to the old familiar coins and legal tender in the form of paper money and bonds and stocks, so long possessed.

A speaker's platform had been erected, safely removed from the scene of the planned conflagration, where Numar, Director-General of the new world government, was to speak, over an international radio network. When the torch was put to the huge stacks of money in Washington—every capital throughout the world was to do likewise—all being synchronized in time for this event, whether it was day or night in foreign lands.

Banks would be open, as usual, the following day, to handle the new Merit currency, on behalf of the government and to issue Merit Checks Books as additional Merit Points were earned and deposited by citizens in the different zones serviced by these institutions.

The Council of Sixteen, with Numar, was to take part in the program, scheduled to begin at eight p.m. A massed band of a thousand pieces and a chorus of five thousand mixed voices were two of the outstanding entertainment features—and the expected audience of a million humans was to be led in community singing.

LIBERATION Day was a holiday, therefore, unique and exciting in the long history of holidays, of one kind and another, on earth. It promised everything in the range of human emotion—from ecstatic jubilation to the uttermost depths of despair.

Mankind had been "conditioned" for the Great Change as much as had been humanly possible, during the three-month period of preparation by press and radio and motion picture—but the New Plan of Living still seemed too fantastic for millions to accept as reality.

"It will never happen," had been the expressed opinion of many. "Something will occur to prevent it. Our governments will put a stop to it."

But now the day was at hand—a day as ominous as Doomsday, which no one ever really expected to arrive.

Late on the afternoon of this day, while Ellen was at home, preparing to attend, with her mother, the gigantic ceremony at Potomac Park, she had a surprise caller.

It was Katherine Barker!

"Oh, Ellen, I'm so glad you're here," she cried. "I didn't dare phone... I had to see you personally. Can I see you in private?"

Ellen led the way to her bedroom, leaving an inquisitive Mother Hopper outside.

"Something terrible is going to happen tonight," announced Katherine, close to hysteria. "I can't reach Andy—he's out somewhere on last minute arrangements with members of the Council—and you and your mother are the only people I know who might be able to get Mister Numar in time."

"What is it?" asked Ellen, feeling her own nerves tighten.

"Ellen—there's a powerful opposition group been organized, which is going to make a last minute try to wrest the power away from Numar and his Green Men and free this Earth from his domination. Some leaders of this group have contacted me - and I've helped them as I could because I...well...I thought they *could* be right...and then I resented your *'in'* with Mister Numar...and Andy's interest in you... I guess I was all confused inside...but I'm thinking straight now. Ellen, unless you can get to Mister Numar and warn him, he and all his Leaders are going to be assassinated tonight and their spaceships destroyed by atomic bombs!"

Ellen clung to the sides of her chair, head reeling.

"You—you're sure of this?" she asked.

"Positive!" cried Katherine, frantically. "Oh, I can see now—when they're willing to stop at nothing to preserve this money system—and all the other things in this world, which need correcting, that this Plan of Living Mister Numar has set up must be given a chance to work. I was told to keep Andy out of the line of fire. When this happens, they intend to put everything into Andy's hands. They're confident that he's the natural leader and that the world will accept him, in all the terror and confusion, and that Andy will have to scrap this New Plan and appeal to all governments to stick to their old tried and true practices to prevent absolute chaos."

ELLEN was sitting rigid with growing fear co-mixed with indignation. "They'd kill me if they knew I was revealing this," said Katherine. "They'd kill you or your mother if they knew you were going to tip off Mister Numar. They feel that anyone who is not for them is betraying the human race—that Numar is probably a dictator, not of nations, but planets—and that we're just his latest conquest under the pretense of helping us. You've got to believe in something, Ellen, or you'll go crazy and for a time I—but I don't know—I'm placing my faith in Numar—

and if I'm wrong—well—I feel there's no hope for any of us, anyway."

Ellen stood up. "That's the way I feel, too… You stay here, Katherine, till we get back. Mother and I are going to the airport and try our best to reach Numar."

The special police officers and honor guard placed around the airship from interstellar space had never encountered a woman like Betty Annabelle Hopper.

"We don't care if you've known Mr. Numar a *million* years," said the Captain of the force. "He's given us strict orders that, under no circumstances, are we to let anyone get in touch with him here. Not that they could, anyway, on account of that fifty-foot safety zone—and Numar never coming or going unless on strict business—and paying no attention to the crowds around."

"Well, can you answer me this?" demanded Grandma Hopper, as Ellen stood by, perfectly willing to let her carryon. "As far as you know—is Mister Numar on board that ship now?"

"Yes, lady, I think he is," said the Captain. "We haven't seen him leave it today yet."

"Then I'm going to see him," announced Mrs. Hopper and marched up to the roped-off area.

"Look out," warned an officer.

"Oh, I'm not going to electrocute myself," said Mrs. Hopper. "I don't intend to see Numar dead, but he'll think I'm raising the dead, before I'm through!" Then, as the astonished police force looked on, she made a megaphone of her hands and started shouting: "Yoo hoo, Mister Numar… Yoo hoo! It's me—your old friend, Betty Hopper! I've got to see you! Something important! Yoo hoo! Mister N-U-M-A-R!"

"Pipe down, lady," ordered the Captain. "George Washington can hear you, clear up at Mount Vernon."

"Mister Numar can hear me, too," said Grandma Hopper, pointing.

The Green Man was now seen to have appeared at the entrance to his spaceship. He emerged and walked down the ramp, through the safety zone toward them, as the police force stared.

"Well, I'll be…" swore the Captain.

Ellen and her mother approached as closely as they dared.

"Sorry to disturb you," Mrs. Hopper called. "But my daughter's got some information she thought you ought to have…"

NUMAR stepped outside the ropes, and motioned to the guards to push back the curious crowd beyond hearing range. He was smiling.

"You are a most remarkable human being," he said to Grandma Hopper.

"So is my daughter," she replied, with spirit. "Tell him, Ellen."

"Mister Numar—your life's in danger," Ellen burst out. "I've just learned there's a plot to kill you at Potomac Park to-night and destroy your spaceship, too. Not only that—but all your Leaders are to get the same treatment abroad—"

Numar placed a hand on Ellen's arm, checking her.

"I know all about it," he said, quietly. "But I appreciate your coming here to tell me. Have no fear. Steps are being taken to counteract these moves. They will not succeed."

"How can you be sure?" asked Grandma Hopper. "You may have lived millions of years…but you're not immortal, are you?"

Numar smiled. "No—but I have ways of protecting myself, which you will witness tonight *if* I am attacked. I want you and your daughter to sit near me on the platform. There will be two places reserved for you. Thank you for coming here. Return to your apartment now and I will send a special car to bring you to Potomac Park."

Numar shook hands with them both, turned quietly and returned to the spaceship. Ellen and her mother did not speak until they had pushed through the crowd and secured a taxicab at the Airport Terminal.

"Guess we worried about him, all for nothing," said Ellen, finally.

"Did us some good though," chuckled Grandma Hopper. "Got us the best seats in the Park for the biggest show on earth."

CHAPTER EIGHTEEN

IT DIDN'T happen until Numar arose to speak, after which he was scheduled to push a button, which would ignite the enormous piles of paper money stacked in a man-made mountain behind him.

The program had gone off remarkably well. All of the Council of Sixteen members had spoken briefly. The huge band and chorus numbers had been thrillingly interspersed and the crowd of about a million spectators, stretched out as far as the eye could see and along the banks of the Potomac, under the stars it was a magnificent sight, especially to those favored few on the speakers' platform.

"This makes up for our disappointment the other night," Grandma Hopper had whispered to Ellen. "In fact, it makes up for all my disappointments in life. You can tell about this to *your* grandchildren."

"I've got to get some children, first," reminded Ellen. "And married before that."

"Well, I should hope so," said her mother.

Ellen was proud, as usual, of Petrov and Andy. There seemed so little to choose between them. Each was a fine leader type, men of high ideals who, now that they were not bound by special interests or instructions from their governments, were working together with true world betterment in mind.

"I really wouldn't know which one to accept if each should ask me to marry again," she thought.

But her decision was destined to be made for her. As time came for Numar to speak and the great floodlights were turned on him, he came and stood before the microphones, a majestic figure in his stately dignity, the white robes, turbaned head, strongly etched green features with high forehead. A veritable god among human creatures, thought Ellen.

Numar began his familiar salutation. "Greetings—all peoples of earth!" he said. But he got no further.

Petrov Gouchevisky, sitting in the front row of Council members, suddenly sprang to his feet, crying out: "Look out, Mister Numar—look out!"

He then ran and dived off the platform, straight at a man who had appeared in the aisle in front of Numar and was pointing a sawed-off shotgun at him.

Petrov's body took the full blast, at close range.

Almost simultaneously, shots rang out from different sections of the crowd—at least half a dozen would-be assassins' bullets winging their way at the white-robed target, so clearly outlined on the front of the platform, behind the glittering microphones.

All was wildest pandemonium but, through it all, Numar remained standing. He did not go down; instead the bullets were dropping harmlessly about him, as though hitting an invisible steel shield, which they could not penetrate. None on the platform was injured—only Petrov who had apparently plunged beyond the range of this amazing defense.

Ellen and Andy somehow got to Petrov's side. Police officers had picked him up, attendants were running down the aisle with a stretcher from an ambulance stationed at the Park to care for any eventualities in a crowd of this size.

"He's dead!" pronounced an intern, after one look. "Killed instantly!"

SOME of the attackers had been caught and badly beaten; others were being chased, Grandma Hopper took Ellen's arm and helped her back on the platform, with Andy following.

"There's nothing you can do now," said her mother. But Ellen tearfully watched Petrov's still form as it was carried through a throng struck dumb with terror and shock at the savageness of the assault upon Numar, its tragic consequences and its amazing failure to harm the intended victim.

Radio announcers suddenly found their voices and commenced excitedly describing the happenings to the outside world.

"A murderous attack upon Numar has just failed!" they cried. "Fired at from many vantage points at once, Numar set up some kind of electronic barrier around him and those on the platform, which bullets could not pierce. But Petrov Gouchevisky, Russian member of the Council of Sixteen, is dead. He gave his life in an attempt to save Numar's, by leaping off the stage onto one of the assassins... One moment, ladies and gentlemen...news is just coming in from other capitals...and we learn that attempted assassinations of Numar's Leaders have just occurred there...all meeting in failure, with most of the would-be murderers caught or killed. Apparently what happened here in Washington tonight was part of a worldwide plot... Yes...yes...it was...for attacks were made on all spaceships but these, too, were repelled by some kind of rays, which made duds of the atomic bombs. Numar and all his Leaders are safe, ladies and gentlemen...the rebellion has been put down and everything is in hand... The huge crowd here in Washington has quieted, although everyone is still discussing Mr. Gouchevisky's untimely but heroic end... I don't know...it looks like...yes, I'm right...Mister Numar is ready to speak to you... Ladies and gentlemen, let me present the greatest figure who has ever come to our earth...Mister Numar of the Planet Talamaya..."

It was a stern and unsmiling Numar who now spoke to his greatly sobered visible audience and unseen millions of startled human creatures around the world.

"My Authority and Power having been challenged," he said, "I must demonstrate to you that this threat to destroy your planet, in the event you peoples do not elect to improve your own conditions here—is not without foundation.

"I now declare to all within the hearing of my voice that within ten minutes from this time of my speaking an earthquake will shake this *entire planet*—such an earthquake as has never been experienced by Man.

"The tremor will be felt by every human and will serve as a final warning to those who would oppose the New Plan of Living."

A great fearsome murmuring went up from the crowd in Potomac Park, which grew into a roar of panic.

"All of you assembled here, remain where you are," ordered Numar. "You will not be harmed if you obey my instructions. Those listening to my voice—do not move. You will be safe if you control your fears. This earth tremor will be controlled by our forces, but it will indicate to you what could be done. You now have four minutes to wait...three...two...one...twenty seconds...NOW!"

AN ENORMOUS shriek shot up as the earth suddenly commenced swaying—a violent tremble, accompanied by an ugly, rumbling sound, which seemed to come from directly underfoot. But the temblor, as Numar had assured, was not strong enough to do more than slight damage to flimsy foundations and broken-down buildings here and there. It did, however, convince all humans, beyond any further shadow of doubting, that the power Numar and his Green Men commanded could not be coped with by any force Man could muster.

"And now," Numar announced, dramatically, while humans, everywhere, were trying to recover from this most shocking of all demonstrations, "the ending of an old, outmoded system and the beginning of a new epoch on this earth."

So saying, he pressed a button and a great shaft of flame shot into the sky behind him. The most costly fire in world history was ignited—touching off other fires all over the planet. Homes, office buildings, manufacturing plants—nothing of value was burning—only stupendous piles of paper! Paper now declared worthless although it had bought in its time all that men held dear and all that men called evil—from the most exquisite rose, to the lowest harlot.

Men and women sobbed in frenzied helplessness as they watched great billows of flame and smoke devour these mammoth mounds of green, which withered and crumpled and turned black and fell apart before their eyes. Others, possessing more faith and no love of money for money's sake, cried out in ecstatic enjoyment of this never-to-be-forgotten sight.

"Isn't it a pity," Grandma Hopper said to Ellen. "I've always wanted money to burn—and there's a heap of it burning—but it's too late to do me any good."

The funeral of Petrov Gouchevisky was placed in charge of the Council of Sixteen. His body lay in state at the Russian Embassy and was later taken to the Main Auditorium in the Foreign Relations building where services were held and Numar spoke a special eulogy.

"This notable specimen of your human race gave his life with no thought of self," he said, in part. "He gave it instantly in seeking to save me that, through me, this New Plan of Living might be saved for your world. Such is the spirit of those who would die for ideals."

Ellen, shattered by Petrov's passing, received flowers and a note of sincere sympathy from Katherine Barker.

"I know you admired him very much," she wrote. "I regret having to confess it but I was the cause of your embarrassment with him on those two occasions. As I look back, I find it impossible to comprehend or excuse my actions, but I do hope you will forgive...K. B."

GRANDMA HOPPER was a great and understanding help to Ellen in the days that followed—days when the peoples of the world, trying out this New Plan of Living, were faltering here and there but desperately endeavoring to make a go of it.

Andy Brownell was devoting day and night with other Council members, studying the workings of the Plan, bolstering its operation, correcting mistakes as revealed by experience, exerting pressure where it was needed, showing consideration where more education and adaptation were required. A new Russian, earnest-faced, blue-eyed Ivan Manski, had taken Petrov's place on the Council and was putting forth every effort to measure up. Things were going ahead and resistance was lessening—both the willful and the ignorant kinds.

Came a night when Andy suddenly put in an appearance at Ellen's apartment and said: "Come on—throw on your hat— I've earned enough points to take you to a picture show."

Ellen laughed. "All right," she said, with newfound spirit. "I will."

They saw the picture—a light comedy—and Ellen laughed some more. It did her good. She suddenly felt so comfortable and, somehow, as though she belonged in Andy's company. Neither seemed to want to turn in just yet and their feet led them down along the lagoon where they had seen the Great Light together—was it years—no—actually only months ago.

"My—the unbelievable things that have happened in this short time," said Ellen.

"Remember," said Andy, "how filled I was of fears about a war with Russia? I didn't see how it could be averted. We both agreed, at the time, that only a higher power could save us."

"And a higher power *has,*" said Ellen.

"Yes—the Plan's working," declared Andy. "Just as Mister Numar said: 'Money has never brought world happiness—nor power; only individual achievement or accomplishment brings it.' And humans now—in every country—are gaining self-respect and pride in the things they are doing. They're not worrying about how they're going to get food and shelter, they don't have to think of stealing or begging to get the necessities of life. Just to think that Man had to go this long before he found out how simple it was to have all he needed to make him happy and let his fellow man be happy, too—without taking things away from each other."

Ellen smiled and pinched Andy's arm. "Are *you* happy?" she asked.

"Well—I could be happier," he admitted, pointedly. "The only thing about this earth that isn't changed is the moon. Have I picked the right occasion and place, this time, to propose?"

Ellen looked up at him. His frank, blue eyes were gazing down into hers. He read his answer there—and kissed her.

The departure of Numar and his Fellow Green Men was sudden and spectacular. He gave no advance warning.

IT WAS the day after his attendance at the wedding of Ellen Hopper, daughter of his "old earth friend," Mrs. Hopper, to Andrew Brownell, one of the most brilliant members of the Council of Sixteen, that all networks were cut off, without announcement, and Numar's voice filled the atmosphere.

"Greetings and Farewell—all peoples of earth!" he said. "When I have finished this last message to you we are taking off in our spaceships to return to our native planet of Talamaya. We leave you with the New Plan of Living under way. Already, countless numbers of you are reaping the joys and benefits of the Great Change. These will increase in abundance as time goes on and you continue your co-operation in all fields of endeavor.

"As you carry-on, a Great Light will commence to dawn in your own minds and hearts. You will begin to sense the Great Plan that God, the Father of us all, designed for this planet and you will expand upon this Plan of Living we have brought to you until your earth will become a true Paradise of Happiness for all.

"That is—all this will happen if you do not again lose your hold upon the gifts of this God-power within yourselves.

"If you do—we shall not return to lend our aid. Instead, having had your last chance to attain Brotherhood, your world will be destroyed overnight.

"To an outside observer, watching from some far-off planet, it would appear that a very small and insignificant star exploded in the Universe."

THE END

If you've enjoyed this book, you will not want to miss these terrific titles...

ARMCHAIR SCI-FI & HORROR DOUBLE NOVELS, $12.95 each

D-1   **THE GALAXY RAIDERS** by William P. McGivern
       SPACE STATION #1 by Frank Belknap Long

D-2   **THE PROGRAMMED PEOPLE** by Jack Sharkey
       SLAVES OF THE CRYSTAL BRAIN by William Carter Sawtelle

D-3   **YOU'RE ALL ALONE** by Fritz Leiber
       THE LIQUID MAN by Bernard C. Gilford

D-4   **CITADEL OF THE STAR LORDS** by Edmond Hamilton
       VOYAGE TO ETERNITY by Milton Lesser

D-5   **IRON MEN OF VENUS** by Don Wilcox
       THE MAN WITH ABSOLUTE MOTION by Noel Loomis

D-6   **WHO SOWS THE WIND...** by Rog Phillips
       THE PUZZLE PLANET by Robert A. W. Lowndes

D-7   **PLANET OF DREAD** by Murray Leinster
       TWICE UPON A TIME by Charles L. Fontenay

D-8   **THE TERROR OUT OF SPACE** by Dwight V. Swain
       QUEST OF THE GOLDEN APE by Ivar Jorgensen and Adam Chase

D-9   **SECRET OF MARRACOTT DEEP** by Henry Slesar
       PAWN OF THE BLACK FLEET by Mark Clifton.

D-10   **BEYOND THE RINGS OF SATURN** by Robert Moore Williams
       A MAN OBSESSED by Alan E. Nourse

ARMCHAIR SCIENCE FICTION CLASSICS, $12.95 each

C-1   **THE GREEN MAN**
       by Harold M. Sherman

C-2   **A TRACE OF MEMORY**
       By Keith Laumer

C-3   **INTO PLUTONIAN DEPTHS**
       by Stanton A. Coblentz

ARMCHAIR MASTERS OF SCIENCE FICTION SERIES, $16.95 each

M-1   **MASTERS OF SCIENCE FICTION, Vol. One**
       Bryce Walton—"Dark of the Moon" and other tales

M-2   **MASTERS OF SCIENCE FICTION, Vol. Two**
       Jerome Bixby—"One Way Street" and other tales

If you've enjoyed this book, you will not want to miss these terrific titles...

ARMCHAIR SCI-FI & HORROR DOUBLE NOVELS, $12.95 each

D-81   **THE LAST PLEA** by Robert Bloch
THE STATUS CIVILIZATION by Robert Sheckley

D-82   **WOMAN FROM ANOTHER PLANET** by Frank Belknap Long
HOMECALLING by Judith Merril

D-83   **WHEN TWO WORLDS MEET** by Robert Moore Williams
THE MAN WHO HAD NO BRAINS by Jeff Sutton

D-84   **THE SPECTRE OF SUICIDE SWAMP** by E. K. Jarvis
IT'S MAGIC, YOU DOPE! by Jack Sharkey

D-85   **THE STARSHIP FROM SIRIUS** by Rog Phillips
FINAL WEAPON by Everett Cole

D-86   **TREASURE ON THUNDER MOON** by Edmond Hamilton
TRAIL OF THE ASTROGAR by Henry Haase

D-87   **THE VENUS ENIGMA** by Joe Gibson
THE WOMAN IN SKIN 13 by Paul W. Fairman

D-88   **THE MAD ROBOT** by William P. McGivern
THE RUNNING MAN by J. Holly Hunter

D-89   **VENGEANCE OF KYVOR** by Randall Garrett
AT THE EARTH'S CORE by Edgar Rice Burroughs

D-90   **DWELLERS OF THE DEEP** by Don Wilcox
NIGHT OF THE LONG KNIVES by Fritz Leiber

ARMCHAIR SCIENCE FICTION CLASSICS, $12.95 each

C-28   **THE MAN FROM TOMORROW**
by Stanton A. Coblentz

C-29   **THE GREEN MAN OF GRAYPEC**
by Festus Pragnell

C-30   **THE SHAVER MYSTERY, Book Four**
by Richard S. Shaver

ARMCHAIR MASTERS OF SCIENCE FICTION SERIES, $16.95 each

MS-7   **MASTERS OF SCIENCE FICTION AND FANTASY, Vol. Seven**
Lester del Rey, "The Band Played On" and other tales

MS-8   **MASTERS OF SCIENCE FICTION, Vol. Eight**
Milton Lesser, "'A' as in Android" and other tales

If you've enjoyed this book, you will not want to miss these terrific titles…

ARMCHAIR SCI-FI & HORROR DOUBLE NOVELS, $12.95 each

D-91   **THE TIME TRAP** by Henry Kuttner
THE LUNAR LICHEN by Hal Clement

D-92   **SARGASSO OF LOST STARSHIPS** by Poul Anderson
THE ICE QUEEN by Don Wilcox

D-93   **THE PRINCE OF SPACE** by Jack Williamson
POWER by Harl Vincent

D-94   **PLANET OF NO RETURN** by Howard Browne
THE ANNIHILATOR COMES by Ed Earl Repp

D-95   **THE SINISTER INVASION** by Edmond Hamilton
OPERATION TERROR by Murray Leinster

D-96   **TRANSIENT** by Ward Moore
THE WORLD-MOVER by George O. Smith

D-97   **FORTY DAYS HAS SEPTEMBER** by Milton Lesser
THE DEVIL'S PLANET by David Wright O'Brien

D-98   **THE CYBERENE** by Rog Phillips
BADGE OF INFAMY by Lester del Rey

D-99   **THE JUSTICE OF MARTIN BRAND** by Raymond A. Palmer
BRING BACK MY BRAIN by Dwight V. Swain

D-100 **WIDE-OPEN PLANET** by L. Sprague de Camp
AND THEN THE TOWN TOOK OFF by Richard Wilson

ARMCHAIR SCIENCE FICTION CLASSICS, $12.95 each

C-31   **THE GOLDEN GUARDSMEN**
by S. J. Byrne

C-32   **ONE AGAINST THE MOON**
by Donald A. Wollheim

C-33   **HIDDEN CITY**
by Chester S. Geier

ARMCHAIR SCI-FI & HORROR GEMS SERIES, $12.95 each

G-9   **SCIENCE FICTION GEMS, Vol. Five**
Clifford D. Simak and others

G-10 **HORROR GEMS, Vol. Five**
E. Hoffman Price and others

If you've enjoyed this book, you will not want to miss these terrific titles…

ARMCHAIR SCI-FI & HORROR DOUBLE NOVELS, $12.95 each

D-111   **THE MOON ERA** by Jack Williamson
         REVENGE OF THE ROBOTS by Howard Browne

D-112   **SON OF THE BLACK CHALICE** by Milton Lesser
         SENTRY OF THE SKY by Evelyn E. Smith

D-113   **OUTPOST ON THE MOON** by Joslyn Maxwell
         POTENTIAL ZERO by S. J. Byrne

D-114   **OUTPOST INFINITY** by Raymond F. Jones
         THE WHITE INVADERS by Ray Cummings

D-115   **TIME TRAP** by Rog Phillips
         THE COSMIC DESTROYER by Alexander Blade

D-116   **THE OTHER SIDE OF THE MOON** by Edmond Hamilton
         SECRET INVASION by Walter Kubilius

D-117   **DANGER MOON** by Frederik Pohl
         THE HIDDEN UNIVERSE by Ralph Milne Farley

D-118   **THE WAILING ASTEROID** by Murray Leinster
         THE WORLD THAT COULDN'T BE by Clifford D. Simak

D-119   **THE WHISPERING GORILLA** by Don Wilcox
         RETURN OF THE WHISPERING GORILLA by David V. Reed

D-120   **SPECIAL EFFECT** by J. F. Bone
         WARLORD OF KOR by Terry Carr

ARMCHAIR SCIENCE FICTION CLASSICS, $12.95 each

C-37   **THE GREEN MAN RETURNS**
         by Harold M. Sherman

C-38   **THE SHAVER MYSTERY, Book Five**
         by Richard S, Shaver

C-39   **MARS CHILD**
         by Cyril Judd

ARMCHAIR MASTERS OF SCIENCE FICTION SERIES, $16.95 each

MS-9   **MASTERS OF SCIENCE FICTION AND FANTASY, Vol. Nine**
         Poul Anderson, "The Star Beast" and other tales

MS-10   **MASTERS OF SCIENCE FICTION, Vol. Ten**
         Robert Moore Williams, "Time Tolls for Toro" and other tales